ENGINES OF LIBERTY
SUICIDE RUN

Suicide Run

Published 2015 by DreadPennies USA, via the CreateSpace platform.

Cover illustration by Carter Reid (wwwthezombienation.com)
Interior illustrations by Graham Bradley

Got inquiries? My Twitter handle is @GrahamBeRad

As of 1 January 2015, this book is not registered with the Library of Congress. I reserve the right to change that as soon as I have the resources, and/or feel like doing so.

Printed in the good old United States of America.

SUICIDE RUN

ENGINES OF LIBERTY, BOOK 2

.   Graham Bradley   .

Also available:
Rebel Heart

DreadPennies USA

"There is danger from all men. The only maxim of a free government ought to be to trust no man living with power to endanger the public liberty."

-Spymaster John Adams

Spring 1772

For Mom, my first fan,

who is always proud to tell people about her "writer son."

(Between the Ph.D/business owner and the firefighter…)

MAITRE KALFU LEVEAU

CHAPTER 1

Fitz was dead, so whether he minded that Godfrey had stolen his badge was of no consequence.

Godfrey needed the badge for the secrets it held; it had resided on Fitz's chest for the whole of his career, absorbing and retaining impressions of magic like a second memory—one that didn't decay with age, or misremember. He'd half-expected the thing to kill him just for touching it, but it had done no such thing; true to character, Winston Fitznottingham had been too lazy to fit his badge with a death curse. For this, Godfrey Norrington was grateful: it would have been exceptionally difficult to fulfill his new mission if he were dead.

Naturally.

He'd spent the better part of an entire day meditating, probing the badge's contents with his mind, seeing what Fitz had learned over the years. He was not disappointed. Fitz had crossed paths with a very powerful sangromancer some time ago, and the badge indicated that it could tell where he was. Perfect. *Guess my luck's coming about*, Godfrey thought to himself. A good sangromancer was rare.

"*Wissung!*" he said, tapping the badge with his wand to cast a compass spell. The badge hovered in his hand, buzzing with energy. It spun, slowly at first, then whipped around fast enough to give a hummingbird a headache. Just as abruptly, it jerked to a stop, its bottom tip pointing south by southeast.

"You're sure?" Godfrey asked.

The badge pulsed once in affirmation.

"How far?"

It pulsed again, nine times.

"Nine what? Miles?"

Fitz's memories floated to the forefront of Godfrey's awareness, showing acres and acres of land that rushed past at great speed until all was a green blur. When it stopped, he saw a murky swamp next to a rundown shack, and he knew the exact distance as if he'd walked every step of the way. Godfrey sighed and pocketed the badge.

"Nine *hundred* miles. Sod all," he muttered. This wouldn't be some casual day trip, and there was perhaps nobody else who could help him like a sangromancer.

Stowing his wand up his sleeve, Godfrey sat cross-legged on

Fitz's carpet and headed south at a full power, using a wind-wedge charm to keep the air from chapping his pale skin. He might have grown bored if he hadn't needed to constantly adjust the other spells on the carpet, keeping it connected to the main source of magic back on the eastern seaboard; enchanted objects like carpets and brooms tended to recalibrate themselves as time went on, but it was still bound by British magic, and Godfrey was at the edges of Nova Brittania.

The farther he flew from the Atlantic Lodestone, the more he found himself muttering Saxon words under his breath to maintain speed. As long as he stayed within the Empire's Merykan borders, he'd be fine—beyond that, any mage was tempting the fates. Nervously Godfrey tapped a finger against his thigh, chewing his lip in thought.

The flight took all day. Somewhere around mile seven hundred, he noticed the carpet's rear tassels coming apart. At eight hundred, the tight-knit edges were unraveling. With twenty miles to go the carpet resisted his reparation spells altogether. Before reaching his destination, Godfrey scarcely had time to jump off the falling pile of woolen threads as it collapsed in a heap on the bank of a murky bog.

"Ugh."

Stretching the stiffness out of his bony legs, he fished around in his pocket and grabbed Fitz's badge. "Where am I?"

The badge pulsed. In his head, Godfrey heard, *Belle Chasse, Louisiana.*

His heart skipped and he spun in a circle, holding his breath so as to hear better.

Louisiana.

Louisiana.

The stupid badge had led him into French territory! No wonder his magic struggled to function—he was too far from Port Atlantis, and the source of every British wizard's magic! The thought of being as defenseless as a common duffer was enough to make his skin crawl. What a cruel price the fates demanded.

He stopped his mental tirade, inhaled slowly, and reminded himself why this was important: someone killed Fitz and Birty. If Godfrey captured this rebel, broke his mind and learned the duffers' secrets, it would all be worth it. Cursing the moment's luck, Godfrey prompted the badge to guide him to the sangromancer.

Another ten minutes passed, trudging through the swamp, before the mossy foliage parted to reveal a ramshackle cabin that seemed to have grown out of the ground. The shack from his vision was there too, but it was not the primary structure of the estate. The place reeked of offal, and next to the main house was a heap of pigs' bones. Fitz's badge pulsed; this was the place.

Tell me more about this sangromancer, Godfrey thought.

He saw fragments from Fitz's memory as the badge struggled to channel magic. A shady figure—presumably the sangromancer—featured in most of them, large and foreboding with a dark presence. Little was known of his origins. Occasionally he worked as a bounty hunter for Mage Corps. For whatever reason, he'd retired to the swamp years ago. Fitz had met the man once, on just one job, and the badge had scant details about it. Godfrey was about to ask more when its magic cut out altogether, brushed aside by an unseen hand.

Godfrey snapped to attention. Someone was home! His whipped out his wand and readied a curse.

"Calm yourself, *garçon*," said a rumbling voice from inside the moss-covered cabin.

"Who goes there?" Godfrey tried to keep his spell handy but between the sudden jolt of fear and his precarious location, he couldn't focus.

"You come so close and don't know who I am? Mmmm. *Tres dangereux.*"

Though Godfrey couldn't see the sangromancer, he could hear the malicious smile in his words. The blood magician's confidence added to Godfrey's discomfort. He swallowed hard and held up Fitz's badge as though it were a shield three feet across.

"I know that you're an elite practitioner. I seek your services in the name of King Charles."

"Then you should present your *own* badge, Godfrey Norrington."

A sooty cloud materialized at Godfrey's left, swirling and contorting into the shape of a man over six feet tall. He had black skin and graying hair that dangled to his waist in hundreds of thin, tight braids. Scars and patterns of ink crept up his neck, and even under his bulky cloak of shredded cloth, his muscles bulged. Beads and small animal bones hung from his beard, and his leering feline grin drove into Godfrey's mind the idea that the sangromancer was in complete control here. The only thing whiter than the swamp-dweller's perfectly straight teeth were his eyes, completely devoid of pupils and colored irises.

Blind, no doubt, but Godfrey felt the man's sight on him.

"You possess youth and great ambition, Godfrey," the sangromancer intoned. "One of those is an admirable quality."

Godfrey didn't know how to reply to that, so he composed himself and tried to take charge of the situation. "What's your name, sangromancer?"

Again, his lips parted and spread into a bemused expression. *"Je suis Maitre Kalfu LeVeau.* You may call me Kalfu."

"'Kalfu'?" Godfrey found it in himself to snort. "That can't be your birth name."

"I took it in lieu of the name that was stolen from me long ago."

"You stole that name from a god of the voodoo religion." Godfrey rolled his eyes and pocketed his wand. "Maybe if this were West Africa I would bite, but I'm too well-read on this continent's history, mate. Tell me another." He meant to say more, but Kalfu's next words provoked silence.

"Don't assume it's only a name, child."

An unspoken power rippled out from Kalfu. His milky white eyes fixed on Godfrey and held him fast. Such power! He'd heard that sangromancers could generate their own magic without a lodestone. It seemed impossible—nobody could *make* magic—yet here it was now, staring him in the face: this magician was powerful in a way that Godfrey couldn't match. He swallowed again, fingers still trembling, and he forced steadiness into his voice despite the rapid-fire thudding in his chest.

"Very well, then. I require your services, Kalfu. You will be richly compensated, and—"

Twin puffs of oily smoke exploded to his left and right. Kalfu disappeared in one and reappeared in the other instantaneously. Godfrey flinched.

"I am blind, and yet I see! You cannot guarantee compensation. You have no wealth to promise."

Godfrey gritted his teeth. "That . . . will change when I finish my mission."

"A weak man buys present spoils with future labors, and only a weaker man would believe his promise," Kalfu drawled, leaning on a staff that he'd seemingly conjured out of nowhere. "I know when you lie. Final chance, *mon petit garçon*. Why are you here?"

Godfrey cast off all pretenses. "I'm in exile. There's a rebel I must catch. If I do, I can return to my homeland, and at a higher station. But I am at the edge of my talents, and I require your services. Satisfied?"

"Ha! That is more like it." Kalfu rested his weight against the staff and held out a hand to Godfrey. "Your palm."

Godfrey extended a hand, thought better of it, and jerked it

I SEEK YOUR SERVICES...

back. "Why?"

Kalfu fixed him with a hard stare that demanded capitulation.

Reluctantly, Godfrey reached out again. Kalfu produced a hair-thin needle and pricked the center of Godfrey's palm, but rather than draw a single drop, the needle extracted a slender line of blood that flowed upward out of Godfrey's skin, twirling in the open air. When it grew to six inches in length, it detached from his hand and floated into Kalfu's own palm, where it seemed to phase through his flesh and disappear. Kalfu chewed his lip thoughtfully.

"Hmm. Very good."

"What was that for?" Godfrey demanded, rubbing at the tiny wound. The skin had healed by magic, leaving a telltale itch in its wake.

"Verification, *jeune* wizard. Blood never lies," Kalfu said. "Now, how do you intend to track this rebel?"

Fiddling through his breast pocket, Godfrey handed over the bottled tracer spell. Kalfu popped the cork off and sniffed its contents. "Clever spell, if a bit feeble. Nevertheless . . ." He raised his nose to the sky and sniffed again. "Yes. Follow the trail to its end, and you'll find him. Claim your reward, and then we will discuss my payment."

A weight sank in Godfrey's stomach. "What? I've already been to where the trail ends. There's naught but the ruins of a battle. The city is razed and its inhabitants gone. If you provide no service, I owe no debt."

Kalfu sighed and shook his head. "Go back, Godfrey. Look

deeper."

A final puff of black smoke marked his disappearance. The wind blew it away, and Godfrey was alone in the swamp.

CALVIN ADLER

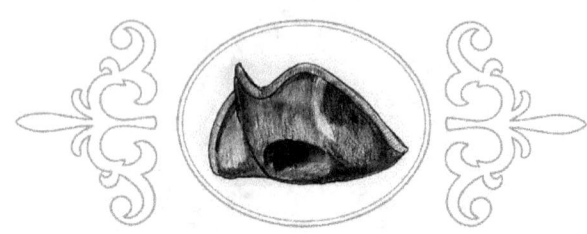

CHAPTER 2

For three days Calvin Adler thought of only one thing at Camp Liberty: escape. When he had secured that, he would focus on revenge.

Peter. Brian. Maybe even John Penn and his crew; there was no way that Calvin was the first person they'd lied to, the first person they'd *used.*

He'd get them. What a cowardly trick, dispatching him like that!

Bitter as he was, Calvin had voiced his thoughts on the matter after arriving, and he'd soon learned not to broadcast too loudly. Hank Duncan, the Rebel Hearts' brigade leader, had told him that a lot of new recruits were brought there under a dubious pretext, but he assured Calvin that they all learned to pull for the cause. Personal grudges were for after the war, and if Calvin made too much noise in the meantime, he'd likely find himself in the brig.

Hank was a nice guy, and honest, and that made it hard for Calvin to dislike him. Still, his words were hard to bear. On top of that, Calvin had gotten his fill of the brig at Mount Vernon, although being down there was how he'd met Amelia.

He wondered if she thought of him as much as he thought of her.

After the war, after the war. Hank's words echoed in Calvin's head. Supposedly the main offensive would launch in under three weeks. It felt more like years to Calvin. He hadn't risked his life and abandoned his family just to trade one tyranny for another, yet here he was. Thus he stewed, studied his surroundings, and watched for an opening.

All things considered, life at Camp Liberty was more comfortable than the weeks he'd spent at Mount Vernon. (For one thing, Hank didn't awaken the Rebel Hearts with buckets of cold water.) There was plenty of work to do, and not all of it involved running or swimming or going through firing drills at top speed. In his first two days, Hank and the others walked Calvin around the base to help him get an idea of the layout—where the mess hall was, where they showered, and where they kept busy by servicing their machinery each day. They told him the meanings of the various sirens and alarms that would go off to announce a returning brigade, a required berth in the medical bay, or mage activity within ten miles of Youngstown.

There was a careful simplicity to it all, designed to keep the technomancers occupied and the mimics battle-ready—in that order.

The work was dull, so his thoughts drifted. When he wasn't dreaming of Baltimore or Amelia, Calvin thought of his friends from Mount Vernon. What had happened to Stitch, Rusty, and the others? Some recent graduates had trickled into Youngstown after Calvin had, but they were all adults. The rest of the new arrivals were transfers from other bases. They filed in, got their assignments, and moved into their new barracks without much fanfare. Calvin kept an eye out for familiar faces, even hoping for a glimpse of Edsel. But no; Edsel had been dispatched to Pittsburgh.

It would be hard to forget Major Tyler saying so.

Days moved swiftly despite the hours crawling by. Brigades usually fulfilled assignments together, so one day while they worked on mimics, Calvin talked with his fellow brigadiers and learned their stories. He was pleased to see that he had a lot to relate to with all of them.

The only female Rebel Heart was brunette belle named Emma Crosby. She was almost twenty, and she reminded him of a more grown-up version of Rusty—a worker and a fighter both, with a sense of calm assurance usually reserved for women twice her age. She came from a family of Carolina fishermen, with parents who were just as complacent as Calvin's when it came to appeasing the mages.

When Emma had finally decided to "rock the boat", she'd hitched a weighted fishing net to a horse and ran down the local mages. With the skill of a lifelong tradesman she'd cast the net, snagged her bounty, and dragged the wizards to the docks, where she ordered the horse to jump into the water. Caught unawares as they had been, the mages were unable to draw their wands and free themselves, and they drowned. Emma had cut the lines from the saddle horn to spare the horse the same fate, and fled the scene.

Her hometown, Litchfield, had plenty of wooded area to hide in, and she made use of it. It didn't take long for new mages to come after her. They were chasing her down when she came across a technomancer safehouse, and the rest was history; Emma had made the cut at Mount Vernon, and was looking forward to winning the war so that she could get her life back.

From the same recruiting class as Emma came the son of a New York metalsmith, Adam Paige, who was second in command of the brigade. His ancestors had been brought to Meryka on a slave ship from West Africa over a century ago. Adam's grandfather had eventually earned his freedom, and spent the rest of his life establishing a good life for his family. His fear of ever being enslaved again had trickled down to Adam's father, making him hesitant to engage in an illegal rebellion.

Adam had not adopted this same fear, and he demonstrated as much when his older sister married a well-to-do gentleman from Long Island. On the night of the wedding, a trio of mages kidnapped and ransomed her. Adam's brother-in-law paid them without a second thought.

That had infuriated Adam like nothing else—were they not

free people? And yet his brother-in-law seemed content to recover his bride this way, like she was just some commodity that fetched a certain price.

So Adam had spied on his brother-in-law during the exchange. Once his sister was safe, Adam followed the mages back to their boarding house and set a barrel of black powder near their front door. He'd fitted the barrel with a long fuse, which he lit, and then fled across the street. From a place of concealment, he began throwing rocks at the house.

"If ever I could have had a photo camera, it should have been that night," Adam had said. "I'd pay a year's earnings to have the look on the mage's face when he saw the fuse at its end. You'll always remember the look of shock they get when they realize that their magic has been completely negated, and cannot, *will* not, save them."

Adam's words took Calvin back to his first raid on a British farm, and the angry mage that he'd blown away with the blunderbuss. The muzzle flash had lit up the wizard's face for the barest fraction of a second, burning his expression into Calvin's memory forever. He hated how it made him a little sick inside, though he remembered why it had had to be done.

The story ended when a TechMan recruiter showed up, returning the money that had been paid for Adam's sister. Adam would later learn that it hadn't been the actual ransom, but a standard recruiting sum paid to newcomers. Calvin bristled at this revelation; it meant that John Penn and his crew hadn't gotten the

Adlers' money back from Fitz and Birty. Another lie!

If Adam's story hadn't been impressive enough, the next one had Calvin glued to his seat. The third Rebel Heart was also the largest, a Danish mariner named Ingvar Prebensen. Endowed with almost inhuman quantities of muscle and long blond hair, Ingvar was the specter of an old world Viking, right down to the battle axe in his arsenal.

Ingvar's family had crossed the Atlantic less than a year ago. While on approach to Meryka, they ran afoul of an unmarked British blockade, demanding documentation for their ship. The captain hadn't acquired any documentation and offered to turn back, but the mages just seized the vessel and all of its cargo. The Danes were to be clapped in irons and placed in labor camps on the shores until such time as they could produce the documents.

"This was all an excuse, of course," Ingvar said. "The mages, they only wanted slaves."

Calvin had figured out that part.

The details of what happened next were unclear—Ingvar sometimes slipped from English to Danish and back—but Calvin had gotten the general idea: the Danes fought their way through the blockade. Their ship, called *Ommerike*, sailed into Staten Island with three dead mages dangling from the bowsprit. The sails had burned, the hull was punctured, and the Royal Navy had to intervene to keep it from sinking in the middle of the port. In the meantime, it took forty-eight mages to quell the uppity (and well-armed) Danish immigrants.

Making do with what they had, the mages had turned the hulk of the *Ommerike* into an offshore jail. Ingvar's family went from sailors to inmates. Word of what they'd done—some true, some not—spread through town, where it reached the ears of John Penn and company. He and his men staged a daring rescue for Ingvar and the others, blasting open the hulk and spiriting them away in a shark mimic.

Heartbroken as they were about the loss of their ship and their property, the Danes were grateful to the recruiters for getting them out. John Penn told them rather frankly that freeing them had compromised their cover in the area, and in return he would need no less than six of them to join the TechMan Army on the spot. Six men were of age and were willing to go, but one of them—Ingvar's father—couldn't perform due to combat injuries. Ingvar went in his place, swearing fealty so long as the army healed his father.

Since then he'd served in the Rebel Hearts as a gryphon gunner. The stock of his blunderbuss looked smooth and well-worn compared to the one Calvin had carried. On one side of the stock, Ingvar had carved a self-designated title, "Techno Viking," and on the other side he had carved the word *Ommerike*.

"Name of this land," Ingvar explained when Calvin asked its meaning. With his accent, Calvin thought he'd misheard.

"You mean 'Meryka'?"

Ingvar frowned, mulling over what English words he should use. "No, the words, *omme* and *rike*, like, a land far away." He made a throwing motion with his hand.

"Huh. I like it."

When it came time for Hank Duncan to tell his story, Calvin expected an equally impressive battlefield tale, given his leadership position.

"Oh, I'm only in charge by way of seniority," Hank said with a shrug. "Been here five years. My family are all sheepherders down in Georgia, and the Brits figured that meant we wanted to feed their gryphons for free. Damn mages kept letting 'em loose on our flocks. Everyone else liked to run for cover when they came by, but I took to watching as it happened, out in the open. Figured that maybe they wouldn't attack if there was an innocent bystander in the area." He shook his head at his past naiveté.

"What'd they do?" Calvin pressed.

"One of 'em came in low and got its talons in me." Hank tugged down on the collar of his shirt to show a long, jagged scar that started at the top of his chest, ran up over his collarbone, and disappeared over his shoulder. Calvin grimaced, imagining the pain it must have caused. Hank went on.

"Worst part of it was that it had a bad grip—picked me up, flew a ways, dropped me. I don't remember much after that, only that some mimics flew in and lit up those gryphons real bad, chased 'em off. I guess one of our neighbors had a connection to the army and called in a favor. Anyhow, they found me and brought me to the surgeons, who patched me up and saved my life. Told me I couldn't leave, neither. Gotta keep secrets and all." He shrugged again. "So I joined the ranks, and here we are."

"Your family knows though, right?"

Ingvar nudged Calvin with an elbow and shook his head once. *"Sore subject,"* he whispered.

"No, it's fine," Hank said as he took another bite. "No, my parents don't know, Calvin. They probably think I'm dead. Guess I'll just surprise them after we win."

A question itched in Calvin's mind, tied to thoughts of his own parents. "How do you do that, though? Doesn't it bug you?"

Ingvar elbowed him again with greater fervor.

"Yes, kid. It bugs me. And there's only one thing I can do about it, so I'm doing it the best I can," Hank said, locking eyes with Calvin. "You miss your own folks too, I can see that. We're in the same boat."

"Well, sort of." Calvin pushed at the food on his plate with his fork, and told them his recruitment story. "My last words with my folks were heated, and then I left and there was a sack of gold in my place. I was happy at first. Now I . . ." he trailed off.

"We know," Emma said, finishing the unspoken thought.

"Like I said: only one thing we can do about it. Win the fight, then you can go shear all the sheep you want," Hank said.

At that, Calvin had to chuckle. "There's a lot about this that grates on me, but it beats scrubbing wool any day."

"Focus on something else, then. It helps if you have some reason to be here, to fight." Hank dug a fork into his eggs.

"I do have a reason, but she's at Mount Vernon."

"Oh?"

I DO HAVE A REASON...

"I . . . it's tricky to explain. I'm involved with Amelia McCracken."

Hank spat eggs across the table, thumping himself on the chest with a closed fist to clear his windpipe. Several heads turned their way but Hank waved them off, catching his breath. Calvin brushed egg yolk off of his tunic.

"Hey! What gives?" he demanded.

Hank covered his mouth, still coughing. "You're involved with *who?*"

"McCracken's daughter. We, well, it's personal, but we . . ."

Hank cut him off with a raised hand, eyes wide. "Not another word. You're gonna cause trouble, talkin' like that."

"What's wrong?" Heart thudding against his ribs, Calvin looked around for some unknown threat.

Hank leaned in and whispered, "It's common knowledge in these parts that Amelia McCracken is betrothed to Captain Hamilton."

INGVAR PREBENSEN, THE TECHNO VIKING

CHAPTER 3

Amelia's eyes burned in the dim pantry. She didn't need much light, as she had the place memorized. Nothing ever changed. She kept it all in order, because that was her duty. Her brothers trained the recruits, they went on raids, they brought back supplies, and she put it all in the stupid pantry. Every. Time.

Stupid to think anything would have changed because she'd fallen for a boy. A quiet sense in the back of her head had warned her about that, even from the first moment she'd let him linger too long in her thoughts. Sneaking him food in the brig, leaning in for a kiss under the tarp, treating his wounds after the painter attack . . .

It could only have ended this way. *Of course* Calvin would have

WHAT HAD SHE HOPED FOR?

left eventually. So stupid of her to get attached to a recruit! They always left, didn't they? And yet she'd hoped that, somehow, he wouldn't. He'd been so different, so real. He'd stood up to Peter and he'd beaten Brian in a fight! He'd been different, and still, he'd saddled up and gone to war.

She'd hoped for at least a good-bye.

Even with the pantry lights dimmed, a shadow filled the doorway. She knew who it was.

"What, Peter?" she asked as she emptied a basket of apples, poured a sack of new ones into the bottom and replaced the old ones on top.

"I heard you crying," her brother said. "What's wrong?"

"Nothing."

"Come on Ames, it's not nothing. How can you work in the dark like this?" The overhead lights brightened.

"I prefer it," she said.

"No, you don't. You can talk to me. It was that recruit, wasn't it?"

Her shoulders slumped. "I don't want to talk about it, Pete."

"I know you don't want to *hear* it, but this is how it goes. He was more than eager to get gone. And he wasn't the first to ask after you, you know. There's always one in every batch that acts the hot shot when they lay eyes on you. That's kind of why Dad keeps you out of sight—soldiers are a little bit barbarian. They have to be," Peter said.

But he *wasn't*, Amelia thought to herself.

"I'm sorry you're sad, I really am. He's not the only technomancer in the world though."

Oh, there it was: the go-to line that they all used when the topic of betrothals came up. The McCracken men could handle all the secrecy and nuance that war demanded of them, but they were as subtle as a brick to the face when it came to her romantic prospects. There was another technomancer out there, all right. Captain Eustice Hamilton was his name, and Dad thought he walked on water.

Amelia would just as soon let him try to, preferably whilst heavy laden with ammunition, just so her family would have to entertain the prospect of her *possibly* ending up with someone else down the road.

She didn't contest the point aloud anymore. Hamilton seemed a perfectly average fellow, if a little violent on the subject of warfare, but he was a captain and that was his job. Whatever it was that her family saw in him, Amelia didn't know, and couldn't care less. Let them suggest and imply all they liked; she would marry only for love, as Mom had.

"Maybe you're right. Just give me space, please? I'm going to bed early, tell Dad not to wait for me at dinner." She replaced the apple basket and pushed past him without another word, retiring to her bedroom.

A short while later, she heard Peter leave the house through the side door, headed for the barracks down the hill. Dad was gone and Brian was out with the recruits, so she was alone. Hurrying,

Amelia shimmied her feet into her boots and exited the house at the opposite end, going into the woods.

Dad parked his mimic in the trees half a kilometer away, under a protective canopy that kept it hidden from airborne eyes. It was a large model with an enclosed interior, and Amelia appreciated the quiet nature of the cabin, the way its silence fostered a sense of safety. She wished that the army had used such machines back when Mom rode with Jack Badgett. She'd probably still be alive . . .

Curses. She was crying again.

Dad wanted her to stay in the house. Peter wanted her to forget about Calvin. Mom would have wanted her to trust her own heart. That was what *she* had done, and it led her to join the TechMan army, despite Dad's protests. The fact that it had gotten her killed wasn't her fault; she'd been a formidable warrior.

Amelia would never be a soldier, or even a pilot in the safest mimic. Dad would never believe she was capable of handling one, and she wasn't about to tell him about her expeditions out here. She knew how to start up this mimic. She knew the controls. She'd studied its schematics and had written up her own basic operator's manual for it. She couldn't defy Dad openly the way that Mom had, but she did have that strain. Amelia rebelled in her own way.

Like Calvin. He was out there. Did he think of her? Was something keeping him away?

What does your heart say? Mom would have asked.

That was the hardest part to figure out: at the moment, Amelia wasn't sure.

EMMA CROSBY

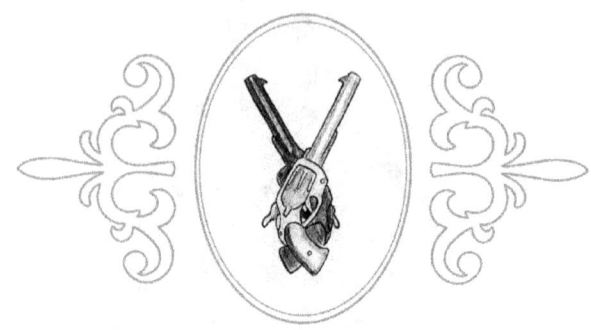

CHAPTER 4

When Calvin would look back on that moment, he'd remember it as the breaking point. He squeezed his tin fork so hard that it folded in half.

"Calm down now, Cal," Hank warned.

"Tell me you're wrong. Tell me that's a sick joke." Calvin's voice trembled. He thought his guts might boil up into his throat.

"Afraid not. Hamilton goes on about it often. He says Commodore McCracken has already given his blessing, and they'll have the ceremony after the war." Hank mopped up his expectorated food with a wrinkled napkin.

A hot rage churned in Calvin's chest, threatening to blow steam out his ears. His parents—like most duffer colonists who'd

36

been relocated—had an arranged marriage, but they were among the lucky few who happened to love each other beforehand. Calvin had just assumed that the technomancers would eradicate assigned betrothals after the war.

Hank went on. "You know most marriages are contracted. That's not going to change anytime soon," he said, as if this would calm him.

"Then what the hell is the point of all this?" Calvin banged a fist on the table. Several heads turned his way.

"We stop 'em snatching newlyweds for ransom," Adam grunted as he drained his glass.

"Better get that in writing," Calvin muttered. A technomancer at the adjacent table still eyed him, prompting Calvin to throw the bent fork. "What are you looking at!"

Hank intercepted the fork with reflexes to shame a cat. "Adler! That's enough. Go back to the barracks."

His tone alarmed Calvin more than his words; Hank was normally calm and quiet. Calvin couldn't help obeying, knowing he'd acted wrongly, and yet he was right to be angry. He got up and stormed off to the tent, hands trembling.

Amelia would have nothing to do with Hamilton, of that he was sure. He was equally sure that he had to leave Camp Liberty *yesterday*.

He withdrew into himself, growing quieter and more reserved with every hour. The others didn't bother him as they went about their duties, save for Hank, who probably suspected something. *Let him.* A plan formed in Calvin's mind, and not even Hank—who could read him well—would know what was coming.

Night came and went. In the morning they practiced repairing mimics at high-speed, simulating a combat drill. Afterward they logged time at the flight simulator, working in pairs on a gryphon mimic. Emma rode with Hank, and Ingvar with Adam; another brigade had an odd man out, Jeb Herbst, so Calvin teamed with him, playing the role of pilot. A few turns on the simulator taught him that gryphons were a little slower than the dragonlings, and not as agile.

Good to know.

Between turns on the simulator, Calvin noticed an office by the motor pool that was always under guard. Worried that he might make Hank suspicious if he asked about it, Calvin brought the question to Jeb.

"HAM radio office. It's how they keep in touch with other bases." Jeb explained how the technology worked, how a user could talk into a "microphone" in one room and another user could hear his words thousands of miles away out of a "speaker."

"Fascinating. Seems like a lot of guards though. 'Round the clock, I mean," Calvin said.

"Radio signals are invisible, but I guess they interfere with magic or something. Like, a mage can trace a signal to the source. The guards make sure that only the operators go inside," Jeb said. "I hear there was a close call once. Someone tried to call out."

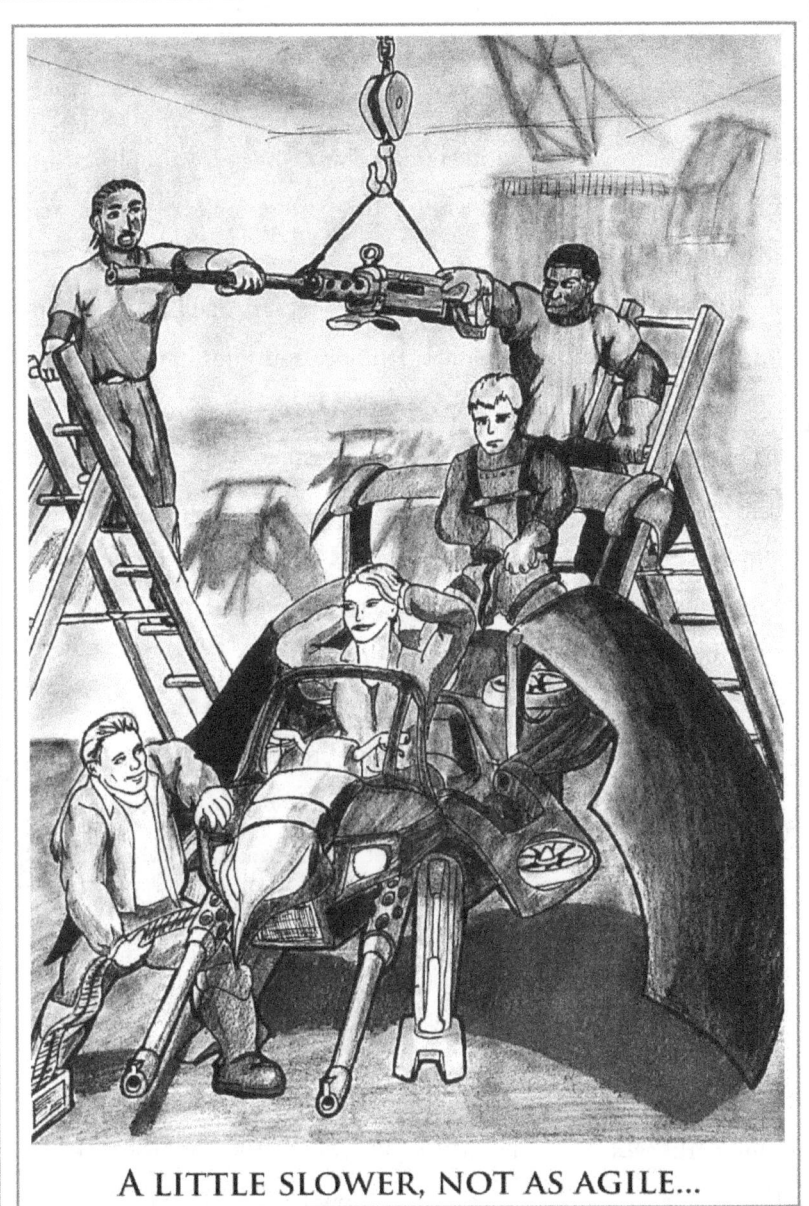

A LITTLE SLOWER, NOT AS AGILE...

"Yeah, can't have that." Calvin hid the excitement that threatened to make his heart explode. Mount Vernon would definitely have a HAM radio, and Amelia probably knew about it. She snuck into McCracken's mimic, didn't she? He would bet his left arm that she knew about the radio. She was cleverer than her father realized.

Adding the HAM radio office to his mental map, Calvin considered this new information. It impressed him that a space so large—bigger even than the grounds at Mount Vernon—could thrive out of the sun. When he'd gotten here, the underground base had seemed endless, but he knew its boundaries now: the primary entry ramp was under City Hall, and it led to the forward motor pool, where techs and engineers serviced them. Beyond the pool, the officers' quarters were to the west, the soldiers' barracks were to the east, and everything in between was either the mess hall, classrooms, training grounds, or life support systems.

The only area he hadn't seen was the lower part of a massive hollow in the middle, and he had yet to meet anyone who'd been down there. More than likely it was the face of the old mine, deep and barren. It bore little relevance to his primary concern: Camp Liberty was a cage, but it wasn't a magical one. He could find a way out.

The day after learning about the HAM radio, Calvin lay awake in the dark, eyes staring up at the canvas of the Rebel Hearts' tent. His mind raced all night, envisioning how he would make it to the camp's front doors. Although their guns remained under lock and key when they weren't training, he carried his knife at all times, fighting the urge to throw it at Captain Hamilton whenever he strode past.

He had an idea of *how* he would pull off his plan. All he needed was the right *when*. His nerves almost got to him half a dozen times, prompting him to take a run at the radio office before he was truly ready, but he kept himself in check. The only thing worse than doing nothing would be to fail.

As it would turn out, Captain Hamilton gave him the final push that he needed.

*

Lunchtime. Calvin sat with his brigade and made casual conversation, talking about how hard it was to change an alternator coil on a dragonling, and how the gryphons would benefit from better balance on the y-axis. He kept one ear turned to the officer's table not far away, where Hamilton sat with a few underlings, some of whom were older than the good captain.

"Been at this for nine years already," Hamilton was saying.

"Serious? How old are you?" someone asked.

"Eighteen. Penn found me in Virginia, been doing it ever since. Literally half my life, you believe that? So yeah, I'm young, but I know what I'm doing. Rank is a matter of know-how, not age. We wrap this thing up, and I'm retiring from the service."

"As a war hero," said one of Hamilton's comrades.

"And the war will be over. All we'll need after that is a force to keep the mages on their side of the pond. I've already got a girl back home to mother my litter and everything." Hamilton drained his glass. "Life is good, gentlemen."

Calvin folded another fork, concealing it under the table when Hank's eyes fell upon him.

"You all right, Calvin?"

"Top shape, Hank."

Hamilton was in for a rude awakening, and soon.

*

That night, Calvin went for it.

He'd volunteered for smelter duty in the afternoon—one of the less-desirable jobs in camp. It involved sorting through junk that the salvage crews had found up on the surface during their nocturnal excursions. Most of it was junk that ended up in the smelter, where it would be turned into other things. The area was loud, the air stank with noxious fumes, and lots of guys got burned if they weren't careful.

Calvin took the duty for a reason: he needed a gun. He had no chance of making one that actually worked, but he figured he could find one that *looked* like it worked. In the end he had pieced one together with zero trigger resistance and a loose hammer, but it would work. Concealing the gun in an ankle holster fashioned from a strip of an old tunic, Calvin finished his shift and began the walk back to the Rebel Heart barracks. Not coincidentally, he'd have to walk right past the HAM radio office to get there.

*

At 10 PM, a grenade rolled down the hallway to the HAM

office. One of the guards' eyes widened and he dived for it, fingers frantically working at the spoon to remove the detonator core. The other guard pulled his pistol on a swarthy figure that appeared in the hallway, but the gun stuck in his holster for half a crucial second.

The attacker clubbed the second guard over the head with a pistol—just to stun him, not knock him out—and pried the guard's gun from his hand. Duly armed, the attacker leveled both weapons at his victims. When the dummy grenade failed to go off, the guards saw their folly laid bare.

"Y'all stay real quiet now," Calvin warned. "You know what happens else wise."

A minute later they were handcuffed back to back, their mouths gagged and their feet bound. Calvin took their keys and unlocked the HAM radio office.

Get in, call Amelia, tell her the truth. Set a place and time to meet, and get gone. It was a simple plan, so he figured there was little that could go wrong. Breathing in deep, he brandished the guns—fake in his left, real in his right—and stepped inside.

Little did he know that his next moves would alter the rest of his life, the fate of Camp Liberty, and the course of the entire continent for all of time.

SOPHRONIA BRIMBLE AND NIGEL SHARPE

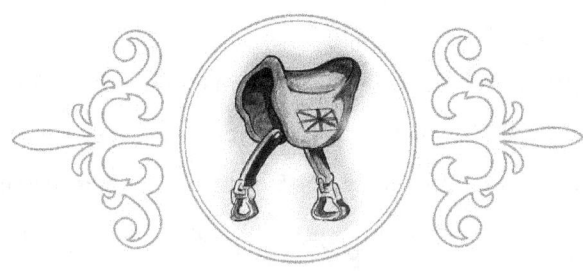

CHAPTER 5

Without a carpet, Godfrey trudged through the swamp until he came across an old witch's shack, from whom he pilfered a broom. Kalfu had had a spare broom, but Godfrey wasn't about to accept a favor from the sangromancer. Some people were like faeries when it came to charity: you could never pay them back for just the act of a loan. You'd have to pay them back for every residual benefit of the loan, which in this case would be every good thing that would happen to Godfrey from now until the end of time, and there was no such thing as cheating a sangromancer out of a deal.

So he hadn't taken Kalfu's broom.

He was still far from the lodestone, but brooms were simpler than carpets. Godfrey nursed it into the air and flew east, enjoying the sense of his power growing stronger. Instead of returning to the Ohio, he flew to New Birmingham, Alabama, where Fitz's badge knew of a bestiary. The owner had lent her services to the Corps in years past, and after dealing with Maitre Kalfu, Godfrey felt he could handle a lowly beast-wrangler.

At most bestiaries, he'd have been right. This one, however, was run by a different breed.

Godfrey dismounted the broom and entered the main building, a ramshackle little structure held together by magic more than by hardware. For example, the wood planks in the walls weren't flush, yet a permanent spell drew energy from the sun outside and channeled it into a shield to keep out dust and wind. The doors had neither handles nor locks, but Godfrey suspected that they wouldn't open outside of business hours, or to any unauthorized patron. And in the front foyer, a wooden fan spun overhead, etched with a clever Saxon rune that made it move faster when the outside temperature rose.

He rang the bell on the counter and dug Fitz's badge out of his pocket.

"Hello? I must speak with the owner of this establishment!" he shouted.

A young lady emerged from the back room, her figure trim and muscular, covered primarily in form-fitting leathers and thin cotton fabric. She wore a leather vest and a black canvas skirt over skintight leggings tucked inside gatorskin boots that accentuated the curves of her calves. She also wore long daggers strapped to either leg. Unlike most faunamancers Godfrey had known, she let her hair grow long, though she braided it in a stiff tail that reached almost to her waist. A bandana covered her forehead and most of her hair, giving her a working-girl image that invited no nonsense.

"Yeah?" she demanded, half-interested.

"Eh, the owner . . ." Godfrey trailed off.

"You're looking at her." She had a lilting colonial accent. Fitz's badge indicated to Godfrey that this was not the same owner Fitz had known.

"Um, hello," Godfrey said.

"Something I can do for you, bobby?" She asked it in such a way as to imply that she wasn't in the mood to waste her time.

"I was under the impression that Iphigenia Brimble was the manager?"

"Aunt Iffie kicked the bucket two years back, din't she? Ain't no warm fuzzy neither, thanks for bringing it up."

"My apologies, I—"

"Yeah, yeah. Anyway, I'm Sophronia Brimble, this is my gig. You got coin or what?" She fixed him with a hard stare.

Godfrey didn't like that; he'd meant to come from a position of power. He'd have to come at her tough, really play the hard mage if he was to get her services. He curled his lip and tried not to straighten up too abruptly.

"Name's Fitznottingham, Deputy of His Majesty's Continental

Bureau of Intelligence." He flashed the badge like he'd seen Fitz do it a dozen times. "I require the services of three fast airborne animals, post-haste. Official business."

"You're a kid."

At this, Godfrey glared. "And a bloody accomplished one. Age matters less than skill, Miss Brimble."

"Oh bollocks, you ain't commandeering my flock, are ye?" Sophronia demanded. Godfrey steeled himself, doubling down on the act.

"In the name of the Crown, yes. You will be generously compensated for answering the call to aid the kingdom in this time of crisis."

"I'd better," she growled, and mumbled something under her breath that sounded suspiciously like *wanker*. "I've only got one other flyer on duty. Can you handle a wyvern?"

"Done it before." Godfrey hoped that wyverns weren't too different from gryphons.

"I have three of them, the rest are out on jobs. Just so you know, this will be expensive." Sophronia folded her arms and tapped a finger on her bicep. Godfrey made a show of considering it before allowing a small concession.

"I'm authorized to offer you one and a quarter times your standard rate," he lied. Her eyes widened.

"Well then. That's a squick more generous than the fifty percent they forked out last time. What'd you say your name was, bobby?"

"Norring . . . that is, Nottingham. Fitznottingham. Winston."

"Right. For that price, I'll even put on saddles. Hop to." She motioned for Godfrey to follow her out the back.

He allowed himself a subdued grin; she'd fallen for it. Then again, being generous with Sophronia certainly couldn't hurt his prospects. Godfrey pegged her for a year or two his senior, and quite the fit bird, for a colonial. He kept his interest hidden, so that she would have time to take an interest in him first, as she inevitably would. *Always come from a position of power,* Father had said. Ironic, yes, considering father's position, but even a pillock could speak truth.

The rear door led to a large wooden enclosure with a high, half-open roof. The floor level was separated into eight paddocks of equal size, lined with straw and the dung of different species. Two paddocks held wyverns, the giant winged saurians that were between gryphons and dragons in size. Whereas dragons had four limbs and two wings, wyverns had only wings and hind legs, with a long, flat tail for steering in the air. They couldn't breathe fire and they were notoriously disobedient on the battlefield, but they could fly great distances on little nourishment.

"Handsome creatures, but you said three wyverns," Godfrey said.

"Third one's inbound. My beau had a dispatch this morning," Sophronia said.

Godfrey stiffened at the revelation that she had a man in her life. He didn't get a chance to compose a response before a shadow darkened the roof-hole overhead. He craned his neck as the third wyvern spread its wings and floated to the ground, landing with a softness that defied its size. At the rider's behest, it tucked its wings and bobbed over to its paddock. The rider dismounted, keeping the reins in hand, and Godfrey got a good look at him. He was a solid-jawed British tar, fully six inches taller than Godfrey, and he sported an impressive collection of scars on his arms and face, augmenting his rugged appearance.

"Mornin', love," he said, flashing Sophronia a bright smile. Blast it all, his teeth were even straight! Godfrey unconsciously pressed his lips together over his own crooked incisors.

Sophronia winked at the man. "Nigel, this is Fitznottingham, of the Royal Intelligence Whatsit," she said, gesturing to Godfrey. "This is Nigel Sharpe, ace faunamancer and the most experienced flyer this side of the Atlantic."

"Pleasure, then." Nigel stuck out his hand for Godfrey to shake, which he reluctantly did. Ugh, he had a snotty London accent—Hammersmith, if it was anywhere. Did this man have anything about him that wasn't worth hating?

"Pleasure, yes. You know what, we might only need two wyverns for this gig," Godfrey thought aloud.

"Oh, but you'll like this, Fitznottingham. Bruno and Lucie here are twins. They can stay linked over thousands of miles. We can spread out and cover more ground with them," Sophronia said as Sharpe made adjustments to his wyvern's saddle.

Brilliant, Godfrey thought. He stroked his jaw as if thinking it over. "Better make use of that, then. How soon could you reach Port Atlantis, Mr. Sharpe?"

Nigel pursed his lips. "That's right close to nine hundred miles from here."

And you don't have to do it on a bloody carpet, Godfrey thought bitterly.

"Should be there this time tomorrow morning, accounting for food and rest. I don't suppose you have an address for me?" Nigel asked.

"House of Commons. I'll send further instructions when we're in position on our end," Godfrey said. "Sophronia, can your Lucie contact his Bruno from the Ohio territory?"

Sophronia looked to Nigel. "Ain't never been that far north, love."

Nigel again calculated the distance in his head, as if he knew the flight time between every location in the colonies. Godfrey fought the urge to roll his eyes.

"Four hundred miles. Give or take. Should be a doddle."

"Swell. We leave an hour ago," Godfrey said.

They flew. Godfrey regretted having to lead the way, as it gave Sophronia a view of his wyvern's posterior, making his inexperience rather obvious. He played it down to being out of practice, fuming every time she corrected his form.

At least he'd gotten rid of Nigel.

*

The animals were fast. They reached Ohio shortly after mid-

WE LEAVE AN HOUR AGO...

night, with only one stop to hunt and take their relief. After landing on a hill overlooking Youngstown, Sophronia dismounted and stretched her legs, while Godfrey tried not to fall over in agony. Damn, but the carpet was looking better.

"What's our quarry, then?" Sophronia watched the wyverns as they drank from a creek at the bottom of the hill.

Trying to ignore the soreness in his thighs, Godfrey took her side and stared at the ruins of Youngstown by the weak light of a slivered moon. This wasn't the same place he'd landed before. It gave him a new perspective on the terrain. "You've heard of the rabble that call themselves technomancers, yes?"

"They're just rumors," Sophronia allowed. "Usually from drunks."

"Unfortunately not. My partners and I were ambushed by one, west of Maryland. Crafty little blighters," Godfrey said.

"How bad?"

"Killed Birtwistle and Fitznottingham," Godfrey said.

"Ain't *your* name Fitznottingham?"

Godfrey gulped. Fortunately it was dark and she couldn't see his face. "Right, I meant our apprentice. He killed Birt and the new chap. Really bugs me, as me an' Birt were great mates. People always talked about us in the same breath you see, so whenever someone says 'Birtwistle' I usually think 'and Fitznottingham.'"

"Oh. Sorry about your mate, then." She sounded sincere. "And you said it was just one? One 'a them popped two of you and got away, and came *here?*"

"Yes. Doesn't feel like he's left, either. Question is, if he's still here, where the devil is he hiding?" Godfrey thought aloud.

"Hold up then, mate. One techie takes on three mages and gets away. Now two of us are here and there's more of him? Just what'n the bloody hell kind of operation is this?"

"The kind where we sniff out this prat from a distance while we can still get away," he said, indicating the wyverns. "Once we know where he's holed up, you signal your boy back in Jersey. Then my colleagues at the House of Commons send in all the wings and wands of King George. Have no fear, Miss Brimble: this ain't my first skirmish."

Her resulting silence told him more than words ever could. He'd *impressed* her.

A few more minutes passed before she spoke.

"To the job, then," said Sophronia, whistling for Lucie.

ADAM PAIGE

CHAPTER 6

"Get out of that chair!" Calvin's voice cracked. The empty gun was steady as a rock in one hand, and the loaded gun trembled in the other. Could the radio technician tell? Would he force Calvin to take more drastic measures?

"I absolutely c-c-cannot," stammered the tech. His name was Ben Kyland. "We're not scheduled to broadcast tonight."

Fuming, Calvin cocked the dummy pistol, careful not to pull the hammer out.

"The schedule is paramount—" Ben began. Calvin holstered the real gun and grabbed a handful of Ben's shirt, keeping the dummy pointed at his face.

"I don't give a dimpled penny about your schedule. I have to send a message. You're going to show me how." Wincing to himself, he pressed the barrel to Ben's forehead.

Ben gulped. "Okay, okay, just . . . don't. All you have to do is—" He cut off mid-sentence and swatted Calvin's hand away. Instantly he was up out of the chair and had one hand on the dummy, the other on Calvin's throat. Ben forced Calvin back against the wall and wrenched the gun free. Quaking with fear, Ben leapt back and turned the gun on Calvin.

The trigger clicked. Nothing. Ben's eyes lit up.

Fear and fury took over. Calvin didn't see Ben; instead he saw the mage he'd blasted with the blunderbuss during the farm raid— his first ever kill. He remembered pulling the trigger and just letting it happen, letting the tool do the hard part at first, so that he could live with the pain of it later. To save his mission, Calvin pulled the loaded gun and fired it up close.

The report deafened him in the enclosed space, making his ears ring. A puff of smoke slithered out of the barrel, and Calvin waved it away to see Ben squirming on the ground, clutching his thigh with both hands. His khaki trousers turned dark red between his fingers.

Calvin's voice was as cold as steel. "I won't ask you again."

Gulping, Ben worked himself into a sitting position. He wasn't bleeding seriously enough to threaten his life, for which Calvin was grateful. He'd have enough trouble assuaging his conscience as it was.

Ben spoke between gasps. "The numbered keypad . . . punch in the frequency there. The black button turns on the microphone.

That lets you . . . talk to whoever you're calling."

"Which frequency do I use?"

Ben grimaced and tried to draw in a breath, shifting his grip on his leg. "You're the one who broke in here! You don't know who you're calling?"

Calvin waved the gun. "I know who I'm calling! Just not the frequency."

With a thrust of his chin, Ben pointed to a clipboard on the wall, with a list of approved frequencies, and the regions they covered.

"Good. Now don't take this personally, but I have to tie you up."

Ben actually laughed. It was a joyless sound.

Minutes later, Calvin was setting the HAM radio to Mount Vernon's frequency. When it was ready, he tried the microphone.

What would he even say? He shrugged and pressed the button. "Amelia? Are you there?"

No response. He waited a moment and tried again. "Amelia, it's me, Calvin. I'm in the Ohio country. Can you hear me?"

The speakers crackled and an angry voice came through. *"Calvin Adler! What the hell are you doing on my radio?"*

Commodore McCracken.

Calvin jumped a little in the seat. "Sir! Your sons dispatched me to Camp Liberty under a false pretense, and I—"

"They didn't send you anywhere you little twit, I did! You're there by my order! How did you get a HAM radio?" McCracken demanded.

Blood running hot, Calvin hit the button again. "You did what? Why?"

"I see what frequency you're on," McCracken said, sounding distracted. Feedback warbled over the speakers. *"I am notifying Major Tyler. You're getting pilloried, boy."*

"That won't work! I tied up the technician," Calvin snapped. "There's nobody else in the HAM office."

"You're an idiot, Adler. Major Tyler has a radio in her own quarters."

Calvin had not counted on that. "Why are you doing this to me?"

"Because you refuse to do your part! You were warned and you had every chance to play by the rules," McCracken hissed.

"It's because your daughter kissed me, isn't it?"

Pause. *"She's done foolish things before. She'll grow out of it."*

That those words could so easily escape the man's lips . . . Calvin almost shrieked with rage. "You tyrant!"

"One brat's tyrant is another man's commodore. Welcome to the war, child."

"You think I'm going to let this happen?"

"You already have. There—I've signaled the Major. Get ready for a long walk home."

Calvin took up the real pistol again, mind reeling, his anger burning like never before. The room seemed to swim around him. "I will make you bleed for this, McCracken." He slammed the gun down on the radio until it sparked, smoked, and shut off.

The time had come to leave Camp Liberty.

YOU WILL BLEED FOR THIS...

Although the sun didn't rise or set for those who never left the base, Major Tyler kept most of the brigades on a dawn-to-dusk itinerary, so the majority of the brigadiers were down for the night. Calvin dashed out of the HAM office, his boots thudding against the stone floor all the way to the motor pool. Jack Badgett's dragonling was not where he left it, but rather on the other side of the aisle, meaning it had been repaired and topped off. The key wasn't in the ignition, as per camp rules. He'd anticipated this, and drew out two thin pieces of metal he'd salvaged from the smelters, thinking back to the first night that he'd bypassed the ignition switch in Mount Vernon's stables.

Whether it was the blood hammering in his ears or the distant siren at the HAM office, he didn't hear the trio of engineers pass by with a loaded wagon, hauling a pin drum for a clockwork giant. Between the siren, Calvin's frantic demeanor, and the fact that he was trying to start a mimic without a key, they made a rapidly astute judgment about who he was.

"Hey!" One engineer abandoned the wagon and dashed over to him. "Get off of there!"

So much for the plan. Calvin drew the pistol and leveled it at the engineer's head.

"Give me the keys!"

The engineer held up his hands, but also held his ground. "Not going to happen. Put the gun down, kid."

Calvin moved the gun to his free hand, then blindly tried to start the mimic while keeping an eye on the tech. When he thought he had it, he took his eyes off the man for a split-second to confirm . . .

A lot happened at the same time. The engine started, the engineer lunged, and Calvin accidentally pulled the trigger. He didn't shoot the man, but a lot of technomancers would've heard the shot. He already heard other guards and soldiers coming in response to the HAM siren.

The engineer's fist landed awkwardly on the back of Calvin's neck. Calvin slashed wildly with the pistol and clubbed him across the face, knocking him down. The other two men had run to join their friend, but they could only manage a clumsy surge when they tripped over his prone form, and then Calvin was jamming his pistol in the holster and revving the throttle. He almost fell off the saddle when the mimic lurched off the ground, and the blowback from the rear booster knocked the remaining engineers onto their butts.

Flying! He went for the doors, ignoring the guards' shouts and demands that he cease and desist. The main door loomed big in his line of sight, and his thumb hovered over the trigger for the belly cannons.

He never got the chance to use them.

A cannon fired. Something exploded. Metal shrieked and ripped apart. The mimic bucked, its lifter fans squealing in protest, followed by a jolt in his stomach as he lost what little altitude he had. The dragonling mimic crashed against the paved floor and Calvin flew over the handlebars, landing hard on his back and rolling for several yards, his pistol wedged painfully against his hip. Another dragonling mimic touched down behind his, and Captain Hamilton dismounted it, his face a landscape of rage. Smoke leaked from the barrels of his mimic's belly cannons, and Calvin pieced it together.

"Trying to run, coward?" Hamilton sneered.

Seething, Calvin drew his knife and lunged for Hamilton. The captain hadn't expected this and barely managed to feint so as to avoid getting run through. Calvin plowed into him and then went down, driving an elbow into Hamilton's throat.

"You! Stay away from Amelia!"

Hamilton choked, and it was the strangest choking noise Calvin had ever heard, until he realized the deranged captain was laughing at him. Pushing hard, Hamilton heaved Calvin onto his back, pinning him to the floor with his superior weight.

"Does the recruit have a crush on my little Amy?" Hamilton said. "Choke on your disappointment. You'll never have her."

Hamilton's fist came down on Calvin's face like a mallet, over and over, each impact driving his skull against the ground. Lost in the fog of battle and desperate for deliverance, Calvin struck back and clutched at something in Hamilton's belt—his service pistol! Hamilton landed another blow, but Calvin jammed the pistol against him and squeezed the trigger. The ornery captain screamed and arched his back in pain.

Heart aflame and blood coursing, Calvin knocked Hamilton aside and got up. The captain bled from a deep graze wound across one shoulder blade. He'd live. Calvin stomped on Hamilton's stomach as hard as he could, leaving him gasping.

"You're done," Calvin rasped.

Voices echoed down the ramp. Calvin almost couldn't hear them for the ringing in his ears. Stuffing the gun into his belt, he stole Hamilton's still-working mimic and flew to the exit. The porters, who had witnessed his altercation with their captain, didn't hesitate to open the doors when Calvin threatened to shoot them. The night sky beckoned, and Calvin emerged above ground for the first time since arriving.

Freedom.

LORD MARNIE CRUTCHLEY

CHAPTER 7

Godfrey had graduated from the Ipswich School in Suffolk, an institution that prided itself on its breadth of magical disciplines. During one term he'd been required to take a class called Analog Sciences, studying the mechanics of the world completely independent from any magic. He'd argued with his father all year long to let him drop out, swearing that he'd never have any use for it.

He'd just have to keep this one instance to himself.

Godfrey cast a screening spell with his wand. At first it generated a cloud of white fog, but when he wiped it away with his hand, the air was clearer than before, and he saw the world beyond through several different hues.

"Say, there's a trick." Sophronia edged closer to examine the many hues on the screen.

"Just something I picked up at Ipswich School. The red patches are warm spots. Yellow means moonlight, and green marks the movement of air low to the ground," Godfrey said.

"And what about that two-toned strip up there?" She pointed at a ribbon of light not far from the wrecked City Hall. Curious, Godfrey traced some runes around it to amplify his focus.

"Bugger, that's a radio signal!"

"A what?"

"Tricky to explain, but they can transmit sounds over great distances. It doesn't just happen, though—it's coming from that . . . oh, what's the word? Antenna. But there's nothing else there . . ." Godfrey trailed off, hearing Maitre Kalfu's words in his head: *Look deeper.*

Could it be?

"Well, we can have the beasties sniff around or—" Sophronia began.

A deep boom cut through the silent night as the weedy lawn in front of City Hall tilted upward, like it was perched on the wing of a huge bird. Thirty square feet simply sliced open to reveal a pitch black tunnel. From its depths, a dull roar drew near to the surface. Godfrey's lips curled into a grin when a technomancer—*his* technomancer—raced out of the gap astride a mechanical dragonling. Seconds later, a pair of gryphon-shaped machines followed, clearly in pursuit.

Underground! That was what Kalfu had meant! Godfrey wanted to smack himself—had he only considered the literal interpretation, he could have signaled for backup sooner.

"Izzat them? Are those . . . technomancers?" Sophronia stared open-mouthed at the three noisy machines rushing through the town. Wasting no time with an answer, Godfrey slapped his palm to Lucie's neck and connected his mind to hers. Lucie maintained a steady psychic link with Bruno, and while Godfrey was still far from the lodestone, he wasn't as far as he'd been in Louisiana. It only took a moment to finish merging with the wyvern.

A splendid whitewashed building came into focus, bathed in magical light even after sundown. He'd recognize that building anywhere: Vauxhaul Outpost in Port Atlantis. Why was Nigel at the Royal Mage Corps headquarters? The House of Commons was next door . . .

Steering Bruno's head to one side, Godfrey realized that the beast was standing in an open courtyard paved with cobblestones, illuminated by magical wisps in crystal lanterns. Nigel Sharpe stood nearby, still in his flying leathers, flanked by a brace of serious-looking mages in red cloaks and bowler hats. Nigel narrowed his eyes at the wyvern.

"There," he said. *"Told you she'd call. Bruno gives me that look when there's another in his head."*

Back in Youngstown, Sophronia shook Godfrey's shoulder. "Hey, what gives? You don't just take a girl's beast like that."

"Hush," Godfrey told her, his eyes shut tight. "Your beau's dismounted."

68

Another mage stepped into Bruno's sight, barking orders to his men. *"What's the bloody ruckus? Get on with it!"* His accent was distinctly Oxfordian, and his voice made the hairs on Godfrey's neck stand up. It was none other than Marnie Crutchley, the High Commander of the Colonial Royal Mage Corps. *Oh, bollocks!*

"Link up to your beastie, then! We're not standing out here for our health!" Crutchley ordered. Godfrey sensed a shift in the connection when Nigel put his hand to Bruno's neck, and he suspected the rugged faunamancer was surprised to feel someone other than Sophronia at the other end.

"Hear now!" Crutchley demanded, looking Bruno right in the eye. *"This ruffian comes soaring in here on orders from Fitznottingham, only we got confirmation days ago that Fitz was killed by a dirty rebel! You will explain yourself and surrender for punishment, impostor!"*

Gunfire erupted down in the charred Youngstown valley. Distracted, Godfrey almost lost touch with Lucie's mind. Were the technomancers shooting at each other? He swallowed hard and licked his lips.

"Lord Crutchley! We're short on time—I trust that Mr. Sharpe has explained our arrangement, and—" Godfrey started.

"Couldn't give less of a damn for your arrangement! Identify yourself!"

"I am Godfrey Norrington, son of Sir Waldo Norrington." Hopefully his father's name might provide even an ounce of clout in this desperate hour. Down below, the two gryphon machines chased the technomancer on his smaller, more nimble craft, but they were still attacking him. "The rebels, sir! I have found their base in the Ohio country! They rebuilt it in the mines beneath an old outpost."

Crutchley glowered and shoved Nigel aside, bonding his own mind to Bruno's. The alien sensation of a distant consciousness sent chills down Godfrey's spine, but he let it happen. If Crutchley didn't believe him, this was all for naught.

It worked. Having seen Youngstown through Lucie's eyes, Crutchley jerked his hand back and barked an order to someone on his end.

"Stand by, Master Norrington! You are authorized to draft a teleportation spell. We'll need a clear beacon to send in the toughs," he said.

"Aye, sir!"

"Crutchley out!" He severed the psychic link. Godfrey released Lucie and exhaled, as Sophronia fixed him with an accusing glare.

"Thought your name was Fitznottingham."

"Sorry. Lied 'bout that, but the rest was true. Steady now, for we are about to be in the throes of battle. You will speak of this night to your children's children!"

*

Calvin cut sideways around a building, then dropped the RPMs on the lifter fans. His landing gear scraped the ground, spraying sparks in his wake. He ducked under a fallen tree and he kicked the lifters back on, clawing for altitude, hoping the tactic bought him some time, but no: the crack of gunfire and the near-misses whizzing past his head told him that the gryphoneers were still too close.

He'd have to take his chances out in the open. The gryphons had larger fuel tanks but they also consumed kerosene much faster than the dragonlings. If he could ride hard and evade their shots, they'd have to turn back for—

The mimic jerked sideways beneath him, and a violent shake robbed him of his balance. One of the gryphoneers had landed a crack shot on Calvin's starboard lifter fan, blowing it to shreds and sending the dragonling into a rapid tailspin.

Youngstown spun around him in a whirlwind of silver and black streaks, halting only when the mimic crashed into an iron carriage. Propelled out of the saddle, Calvin slammed ribcage-first into the top of a bench and met the ground with his face. For several long seconds he couldn't feel his nose. When sensation returned, a roaring pain hit him like a stampeding boar, and he tasted blood.

The gryphons landed behind him, thudding onto the broken pavement. Their gunners dismounted with rifles in hand. More footsteps, and Calvin counted four infantrymen charging through the wreckage as well, training their sights on him.

"Don't shoot! The Major wants him alive," someone said.

Rough hands yanked Calvin to his feet. He tried not to cry, biting back tears for both the pain and the futility of the fight. He would never be free. Whatever mystic forces bestowed liberty on mankind had decided that it just wasn't for him, no matter what he did.

They patted him down and relieved him of both pistols. A foot soldier slipped handcuffs onto Calvin's wrists and dragged him over to one of the gryphons. Calvin stared at the menacing mimic, wondering how he might escape this time, knowing that it was impossible, that he'd never see home again, never see Amelia . . .

Overhead a thick black cloud suddenly burst into being. Lightning touched down in a wide radius around the city, and thunder boomed so loud that the very night ripped open. It was so powerful, so abrupt, that a few of the technomancers dropped their weapons in alarm, even as a hole appeared in the air and two wyverns flew out of it, each carrying a human passenger.

Calvin crouched behind a TechMan who'd kept his wits and trained his rifle on the invaders. One rider was a girl wearing riding leathers, and the other was a younger man in the robes of a mage. Something about him looked familiar but Calvin didn't have time to identify him, because in their wake came a veritable army of mages, one hundred strong or better. They surged in on beasts and brooms and carpets, wands in hand and curses on their lips.

"Enemy incursion!" yelled one of the foot soldiers.

"They're not supposed to be able to reach us here!" said another.

"You tell them that!"

Gunfire peppered the sky, drowning out the rest of their words. The mages instantly retaliated with a shower of multi-colored sparks—volatile curses that rained down like fire. Some hit the infantrymen, killing them instantly. Other shots went wide. From the ground, one soldier caught a mage in the chest and unseated him from his broom.

Valiant as the effort was, the mages had the element of surprise as well as superior numbers, and the amount of brightly-colored curses jetting from their wands was greater than the bullets that cut through their ranks.

In the confusion, Calvin escaped custody and ran for what meager cover he might find.

The two lead wyvern riders immediately set onto the gryphon mimics that had just taken to the sky anew. Grateful to be forgotten, Calvin disappeared into the shadows, handcuffed and unarmed, watching in awe at the horror above. Once the last of the skyfaring troops came through, the mages' portal sank down to ground level and disgorged a second army. Calvin saw warg-riders, real gryphons, and trolls dragging huge stone clubs.

Deep, primal fear triggered every nerve in Calvin's body. His hands went clammy and his knees wobbled; he had to lean against an aged tree to stay upright. Maybe he should run, but where? The wizards spread out everywhere, not that they needed to: they could cast spells or use potions to enhance their senses, maybe even see him in the dark the way a tree cat saw its prey. One mage scribbled out a terramancy equation in the dirt, a truly frightening prospect to Calvin's mind: if they used those equations to see everything within a certain area, would they be able to see the base underground?

Until the mage army arrived, Calvin wouldn't have thought it possible to sink to an even deeper level of hopelessness.

And yet, if he could say one thing about the technomancers, it was that they would not go quietly into the night. Trapdoors all around the city slammed open, emergency sirens blaring from their depths. In full strength, the TechMan army answered the mages' sudden arrival. Gunfire cracked repeatedly, an off-tempo chorus of explosions that intensified as their numbers grew. Mages tumbled from their brooms, and their beasts howled in anger. The wizards replied by casting huge, powerful spells that worked their influence over whole areas, ensnaring the fully-armored TechMans and slowing them down.

Already, the stench of blood was strong.

Calvin had to get out of these cuffs. Unfortunately the gryphon riders all wore the same uniforms and armor, so he had no idea who it was that had cuffed him. Were the keys universal?

Keys. Maybe he didn't need them. Did handcuffs and ignitions have similar tumblers? He squatted down and slipped his wrists under the curve of his butt, breathing deep so that the throbbing pain in his face wouldn't overwhelm him. At least the nosebleed has stopped, though it had caked blood on his lips and chin.

To speed up the process, he dropped into a sitting position and worked his feet through his arms to get the cuffs in front of him. The frosted iron knife was still at his ankle. He plucked it out and tried to angle the tip into one keyhole, but the task was harder than he'd anticipated. The hole was small, the knife point was big, and he couldn't grip it well with his hands bound.

The battle got louder. More wizards came through the portal

with monsters in tow, wreaking instant havoc. In reply, the technomancers sent wave after wave of mimics up from the motor pool, turning the sky into a landscape of chaos. The boom of black powder mixed with the multi-colored insanity of the curses, breaking broom and beast and mimic alike. Bodies rained down into the streets, where they were trampled by lumbering trolls or clockwork giants, clamoring to knock each other out on the ground. Calvin might have imagined fights like this since joining the army, yet experiencing it was more than his dreams could have shown him.

It was horrifying.

He cursed as the knife tip broke off in the key hole. It was no use: he needed the keys. One of the gryphoneers had fallen several yards away, his body ensnared by magical vines that had likely strangled him. Brandishing the knife, Calvin loped into the open with designs on cutting the vines and going through the man's pockets.

Ain't nothing else for it! Go!

As soon as he emerged, a witch flew by on a rug and flung a curse at him. It hurtled straight and true, a beam of reddish-blue light that nearly blinded him; he slashed at it with the knife, more out of desperation than anything else, and the beam veered off course, striking the ground harmlessly.

Frosted iron, he thought, pausing for the briefest moment to consider what had just happened. The metal could still foul the magic! He clutched the knife tighter as the witch circled back around for another pass, shrieking in Saxon. Calvin froze, unsure if he could duplicate the feat . . .

. . .but he didn't have to. Two gryphon mimics converged on the witch at a speed he wouldn't have thought possible. One gunner shredded her carpet, ruining the spell that gave it flight, and the other one sprayed bullets through her robes. The witch plummeted to the ground and skidded to a halt in a heap of ash and soot.

The first gryphon landed in front of Calvin. The pilot—a brigade leader—removed his helmet. It was Hank!

"Calvin, what are you doing?"

"Just waiting for a ride, Hank!" Mercy, but they had good timing! He sprinted to the gryphon and held up his hands, hoping they had keys. Hank narrowed his eyes as Emma, the gunner, swept the area around them. The other gryphon zipped past, carrying Ingvar and Adam, who continued the work of death against the encroaching mages.

"Why are you cuffed?" Hank demanded.

"Long story. Can you spring me?" Calvin thrust out his hands again. Muttering under his breath, Hank swatted at his pockets, stopping when Emma brought the gun around and let loose on an incoming wyvern. The winged giant screamed as Emma traced a line up its exposed belly, yet the force of her firepower couldn't slow its massive bulk. Hank shoved Calvin aside as the wyvern belly-flopped against the ground and rolled into the gryphon at speed, knocking it over and smashing it. They skidded a few yards away and the wyvern collapsed atop the wreckage. Emma had been thrown from the gunner's perch, and Hank was nowhere in sight.

"Hank!" Calvin cried.

"Calvin, help me!" Emma was already up, trying to lift the wyvern's wing. Calvin joined her, but it still proved too heavy for the pair of them. Then Emma gasped in pain as a bright blue stunning spell struck her in the chest and threw her onto her back. Calvin flinched, wrists still bound, whirling with his knife in search of the attacker. As it turned out, it was the wyvern's rider.

"Oh I'll do you for that, you duffer rabble!" said the mage as he untangled himself from the saddle. "I have a feeling Sophronia liked this one."

Calvin positioned himself between Emma and the mage, jealously eyeing the pistol in her holster. He nudged her with his toe.

"Come on, Emma! Get up!"

The mage rolled down the wyvern's wing and landed lightly on his toes, pointing his wand at Calvin. "Drop the knife, you sod."

"You can piss right off," Calvin snapped, sounding much braver than he felt.

"Right! Not likely." The wizard hurled a spell. Calvin slashed, and the knife's protective aura cut the bolt of light in two. Bright orange flames seared his forearms but the magical fire died out quickly, impaired by its contact with the forbidden metal.

"Ain't that a cheap trick," the wizard sneered. "You're worth more alive, but I'll off you if I must."

77

Bradley

79

"Who are you?" Calvin demanded. The battle still raged across the city, and yet he felt obligated to ask. There was something . . . fishy about this one.

"I am Godfrey Norrington, your personal headhunter. You killed my partners out in the woods, so I followed you and found your hideout. All this?" He gestured to the portal and the still-growing mage army. "*My* doing. I can't imagine how well my fortunes will change after I personally hand you all over to Crutchley. They might even name a colony after me—"

When the mage looked wistfully into the sky, Calvin struck. He covered the distance and stabbed at Godfrey's wand hand, causing him to retreat and stumble over the wyvern's wing. Unfortunately, Calvin tripped as well and they both went down. The wand and the knife were lost as they grappled hand-to-hand, a class wherein Calvin was clearly the better fighter.

Mages never got their hands dirty, after all.

When they came to their feet, Calvin stood behind Godfrey, pulling the handcuffs tight against his throat. The mage's face darkened in the moonlight as he tried to get free. Calvin only doubled his efforts, squeezing so hard that the cuffs drew blood from his wrists.

"We duffers do your heavy lifting, and who gets stronger?" Calvin spat. "I've wrestled goats that put up more of a fight. You Brits and all your superiority, pah! Take away the wand, and see what happens?"

Then Godfrey threw his weight forward and fell to his knees, taking Calvin down with him; the mage pulled free, unharmed, if a little red around the neck. He recovered his wand as Calvin got up, but he had trouble mustering the breath to utter a curse. Still, he managed something, and the tip of his wand brightened . . .

CRA-BOOM!

A very close gunshot went off. Godfrey screamed in pain and clutched at his ribs. Calvin jerked his head toward the sound and saw that Hank had pulled himself halfway out from under the wyvern; smoke issued forth from his revolver.

"Them lungs ain't so useful once they pop!" Hank taunted. He cocked back the hammer for a second shot, but Godfrey had already trained his wand on Hank. This time he was able to get out a full curse.

"CEORFAN!"

A burst of light sliced Hank's hand clean off, causing blood to fan out around his forearm. The gun clattered away and Hank roared, clutching at the wound, eyes fixed on his severed hand, the pistol still gripped tight.

Calvin and Emma screamed a unified *"No!"* Godfrey again took notice of Calvin and, still cradling his ribs, aimed his wand at him, sneering as blood trickled out of his mouth. With an immutable sense of impending doom seizing him, Calvin could only stare at the wand's glowing tip and think that this was it, he was going to die this time.

Once more he was saved by interrupting gunfire, courtesy of Adam and Ingvar. Bullets chewed up the ground between them, kicking up ash and dust. Instead of casting his spell, Godfrey coughed and raised his hand to cover his face, an act that could only be self-preservation.

From the dust?

A memory stirred in Calvin, the faintest echo of a half-heard conversation between two techs in the motor pool that week. He'd been cleaning soot out of a gryphon's intake, discarding the ash in a bin, and one of them said...

"Shame we can't sort this stuff out. Half of it is frosted iron anyway. Like tossing gunpowder."

Yes! John Penn had mentioned that too, right after Calvin arrived. Technomancers had pumped the dust up to the surface to make it lethal for the mages to invade the area. The very ground he stood on was a weapon!

Adam brought his gryphon down low, banking hard to shed speed. Ingvar, the insane Techno Viking, bailed off of the gunner's perch and hit the ground in a perfect tuck-and-roll. As he took off running, he produced his prized battle axe and barreled toward Godfrey with a Danish war cry on his lips.

Helplessly, Calvin watched as his fellow Rebel Heart assaulted a full mage with nothing but a stick and a sharp blade. Godfrey staggered and slashed his wand through the air to form quick, crude defensive wards. Ingvar's axe bounced off of the air between them yet he still drove Godfrey back.

"Ingvar, be careful!" Emma cried.

"Get Hank!" Ingvar bellowed back.

As they quarreled, Calvin's eyes darted all about. He needed his knife! If he had it, he could come at Godfrey from behind and finish him off. Keeping one eye on the Techno Viking, Calvin kicked around for his lost weapon. As Godfrey's shield spells grew weaker, the mage fished a vial out of his pocket. Before Calvin could guess what it was, Godfrey popped the cork and drank its contents; instantly he straightened up with a renewed vigor and released his injured side. Damn, it was a healing potion! He thrust his wand at Ingvar and formed a more powerful shield-dome between them, then uttered a Saxon curse.

"Anweald scur!"

Out of nowhere, a gale-force wind threw Ingvar off of his feet and smashed him hard against the dead wyvern. His battle axe skittered away and magically morphed into a long, wet, rancid fish. Ingvar wasn't even conscious to see it.

His knife! Calvin saw it glint in the moonlight, and snatched it up. Now or never: he rushed at Godfrey while he was still focused on Ingvar. Calvin would go for the neck; even if it wasn't a killing blow, it would hurt Godfrey, allowing Calvin to line up a second strike. Godfrey drew in a breath and repeated the first half of the curse that had sliced off Hank's hand. Calvin leapt at him, arms outstretched.

"CEOR—"

The ground heaved with impossible force, cutting his curse short and bucking them all into the air. Calvin collided with Godfrey and they both ended up sprawled out on the ground, unsure of what had happened. Explosions ripped up the streets for several blocks, and what Calvin had initially thought were gryphon bombs turned out to be something else:

Trapdoors. *Big* ones, and lots of them. All over town, huge hatches the size of a house blasted upward, exposing Camp Liberty below and disgorging the rest of the TechMan arsenal.

Calvin rolled sideways with the new curve of the ground. The dead wyvern and the wrecked mimic slid away too, following the downward grade. Emma tried to keep Hank from disappearing down a sinkhole, and Adam expertly flew his gryphon into a brand-new chasm, catching the comatose Ingvar on the gunner's platform.

Okay. They were okay. Couldn't worry right this second, Calvin had to make sure Godfrey was dead or dying! He jumped to his feet, scanning the area for the mage but failing to spot him. Most of Youngstown had just fallen into the ground—had he been swallowed up?

Through the diminishing roar of engines and gunfire, Calvin's ears pricked toward the sound of Emma's voice. She was by her mimic, tearing part of her shirt to make a tourniquet for Hank's wrist. Calvin stood frozen in place by anguish, his mind numb, wanting to help his friend but unable to make his feet move.

Then he felt it.

In the week that he'd been at Camp Liberty, he'd come to recognize the hum of a machine running, and he could tell different ones apart based on how they sounded, or how they could vibrate the very air around them as they idled. Well, there was definitely a machine running now, and judging by the feel of it, it was a few dozen times larger than anything he'd touched. He soon matched sight to sound when it rose up out of the massive hole in the earth, and the specter of it shocked him breathless.

The monstrosity was nearly half the size of the entire base. To hide something of that magnitude, it had to have come from the abyss in the center of the mine. There was no other way to contain something so massive! It could have fit Mount Vernon's mansion, stables and dormitory inside its belly, and that wasn't counting the wings with their eight lifter fans, the four gigantic thrusters tucked against its sides, the thick snakelike tail, or the dozens of guns and cannons that bristled all over its body.

A dragon. The technomancers had mimicked a dragon.

Even the mages stared in awe at the twelve-hundred-foot long machine floating ninety feet off the ground, kicking up a cloud of frosted iron dust. The mimic's elaborate head was the work of fine artists, every bit as fearsome as the head of a real dragon. A long, forked tongue protruded from its maw, like a reptile constantly tasting the air. The armored sections of the neck led back to the main body. Calvin couldn't even guess how many crew members were necessary to operate it.

As the largest mimic in history extricated itself from the collapsed mine, it planted its legs, spread its wings wide, and *tick-tick-ticked* all over, the sound of a hundred guns chambering their rounds. Upon the breast of the mighty mechanical beast, the words

rounds. Upon the breast of the mighty mechanical beast, the words *Saint George* were stamped into the metal, alongside a dramatic rendition of George Washington.

Calvin snapped out of his trance when the *Saint George* opened fire on the thick of the mage army, spitting ammunition in every direction. The sound was like dueling thunderstorms, a poorly timed chorus of *boom-boom-boom* that filled the air with fast-moving lead. As Calvin dropped down and plugged his ears, shadows danced rapidly in the light of the muzzle flashes, and empty casings as thick as two fingers clanged against the pavement.

Trolls, wargs, and gryphons fell like wheat to the scythe. What remained of the TechMan army rallied at the feet of the *Saint George*, adding their guns to the onslaught.

To Calvin's chagrin, both armies retreated. He expected the mages to flee in the face of the *George's* awesome firepower, yet he had not expected the other TechMans to turn tail—until he saw them using the appearance of the *Saint George* to cover their escape. The officers' haste suggested that the mages were not supposed to see the dragon mimic just yet.

Adam circled back around a final time and touched down beside Emma and Hank. The Techno Viking was awake but prostrate on the gunner's perch, blunderbuss in hand, trained on the mages' portal. Sharpshooters aboard the *Saint George* still picked at the escaping enemies, enjoying what small victories they could.

"Greenhorn, get moving!" Adam said to Calvin. He and Emma were lifting Hank onto the already overloaded vehicle.

Calvin didn't reply. He just stared at the *George*, at the new damage done to Camp Liberty, and at his injured friends. Something told him it wasn't coincidence that he was followed here by the same mage that he'd failed to kill in the woods a few weeks ago . . . but how could they have followed him? Magic alone?

If they could find him here, under a layer of frosted iron dust at the extremes of New Britain, what hope did he truly have of ever escaping the reach of the Crown?

A crushing weight struck his heart. Not a physical weight, but the sensation took his legs out from beneath him all the same, and he collapsed to his knees in the swirling dust. Mages flew to the portal, technomancers flew away.

All this power, all these cannons, all these engines, and this is the best we can do. A mutual retreat.

The despair of it crippled him. The technomancers had prepared this assault for years, building a massive secret arsenal. They could have used it to great effect if it had stayed a secret.

But it hadn't.

Because of him.

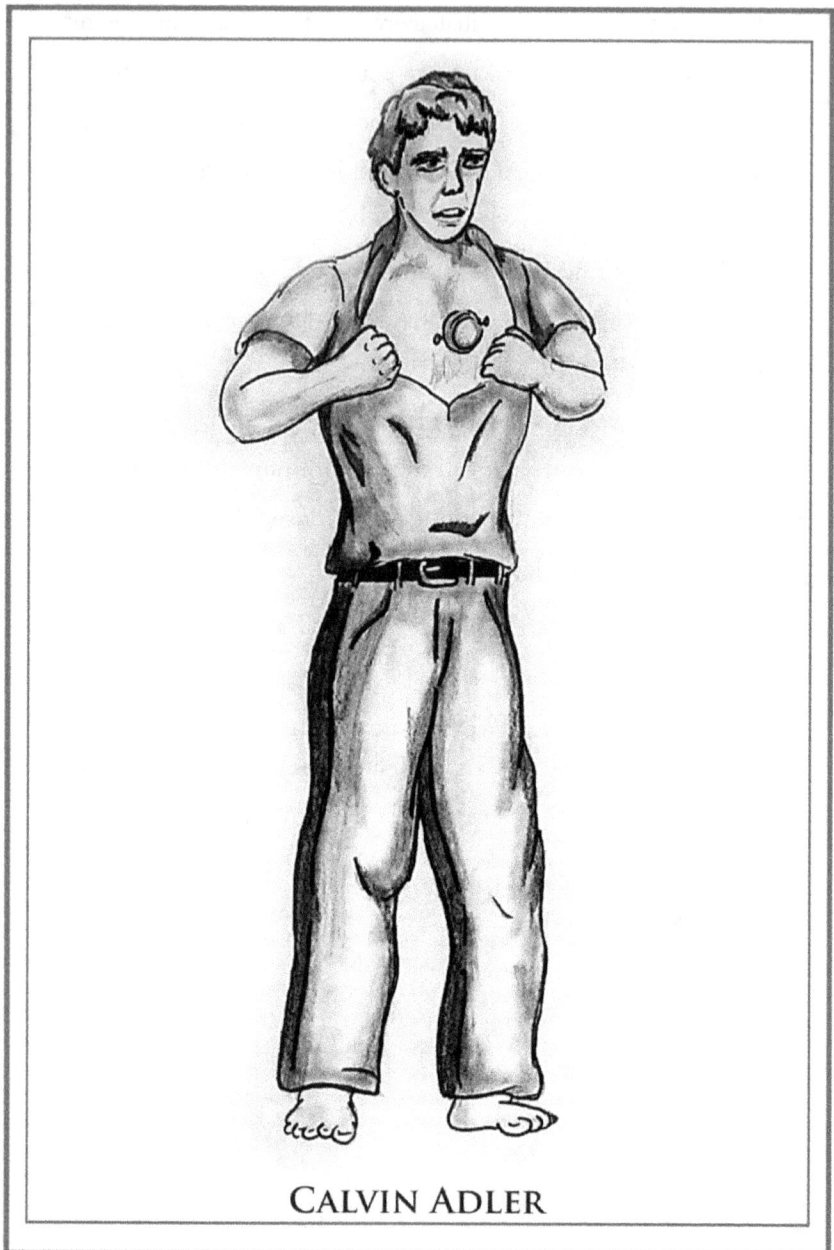

CALVIN ADLER

CHAPTER 8

Never in his life had Godfrey fled anything with such haste.

When the duffers' dragon had first joined the fight, he felt the initial disgust that came with seeing the "technomancers" trying to pass off their tinkering as actual magic. But that disgust evolved into sheer terror when the machine put its awesome firepower on display, and Godfrey's contempt would not make him bulletproof. Cut off from his target, unarmed, and covered in poisonous dust, Godfrey did what was prudent: he scampered.

His wyvern was dead and Sophronia was gone. He'd picked up a discarded broom and raced back to the teleportal, uttering a quick incantation to make sure he didn't come out with the rest of the toughs. The magical teleportation corridors were under steady surveillance so that the French and Spanish mages wouldn't try to use them to invade, but Godfrey knew his way around the network. After all it was his father, Sir Waldo, who monitored the grid in England. Godfrey had been hesitant to tap into it here in Meryka, but the situation demanded it. He'd just have to trust his magic to keep him clandestine.

Without his wand, Godfrey had trouble focusing his magic with pinpoint accuracy; as such, he exited the teleportal miles away from Kalfu's shack in Louisiana. The broom, which had already been damaged when he'd picked it up, fell to pieces after enduring such abuse in combat. The distance from the lodestone wasn't helping much either. Suddenly, Godfrey was on his feet again, robes torn and soiled, forced to walk like some stupid duffer.

Despite it all, there was a positive: Kalfu had been right about Adler's whereabouts, and right now he was the only asset Godfrey had left.

So Godfrey walked. And he went south.

*

Triumph and failure rolled into one: that was the mood of the Camp Liberty technomancers as they plowed through the wilderness toward Pittsburgh. Triumph, for their creation had repelled a magical attack at nearly full strength, yet failure because they had surrendered the element of surprise. The *Saint George* was not meant to have made its debut for two more weeks, during the primary offensive.

Now the mages at least knew what they were in for, and they could prepare. Most of them had made a run for it, leaving very few of their comrades behind after the teleportal had closed. Survivor stories would reach Port Atlantis. Years of preparation, of blood and sweat and tears, were all wasted.

Calvin was almost grateful for the anxious haste with which thousands of men and women moved across the countryside, sticking to dangerous routes through Indian territories to make their road. As long as Major Tyler was focused on getting her army safe (though no place could conceal the *Saint George* now), she couldn't focus her anger on Calvin.

That wasn't to say that word hadn't reached his ears that Captain Hamilton was looking for him; it just wasn't as high a priority.

The other Rebel Hearts were decent enough not to say anything about it, and he kept to himself as he worked with them, tending to Ingvar and Adam's gryphon mimic. Emma had commissioned another one from the motor pool—Camp Liberty had an excess of machines—and Calvin did his part to move it along on a four-wheeled cart through the woods. He said nothing, ate half rations, and slept under the cart at night at Adam's suggestion.

He didn't get much sleep. On top of everything else that had gone wrong, he couldn't stamp out the burning guilt in his heart over what had happened to Hank's hand. Mimic throttles were universally right-handed; even if they switched him to the gunner's spot, firing with his off-hand would be cumbersome. Calvin had no idea how Hank would break the news to Major Tyler, that he was no longer fit to operate mimics. Like Calvin, Hank kept to himself, curled up on the gunner's perch most nights, his stump of a hand tucked under his other arm inside a long jacket. For now, nobody outside their brigade had noticed what happened to him.

They trekked for thirty-eight hours straight on an unforgiving course, stopping only for brief repairs and water breaks. Twice they fitted the *Saint George* with makeshift ballast and floated it downriver when the water was too deep. On one occasion they had to activate its lifter fans and fly it a short distance. Finally, they reached Camp Monroe, west of Pittsburgh. As hard as the trek had been, most of the technomancers were glad to have escaped detection and further harassment by the mages.

"That's good," Ingvar said when the chatter reached their brigade.

"And bad," Adam countered. "If they had the resources to follow us, they would have. That means we only repelled most of what they had here in Meryka."

"How's that bad?" asked Calvin, daring to speak up.

"Now they'll call for reinforcements, kid. And they'll ask for even more than what they lost," Emma said. "We won't be able to stay here for long. We'll have to keep moving the *Saint George* until we're ready to attack."

"Whole damn thing just got a lot harder," Adam grumbled. He didn't stare at Calvin, but Calvin knew what he was thinking.

They set up camp without getting too comfortable. The area

was lush with foliage and laced with rivers; unlike Youngstown, the Pittsburg base was dug shallow due to the high water shelf. Most buildings were on the surface, disguised as storehouses. Supposedly Major Fox Glenshaw of Camp Monroe served double duty as a pro-mage duffer on the city council, and the buildings were under his jurisdiction. He kept the mages from investigating too closely, and with good reason: they'd interrogate and execute him if they knew he was a technomancer.

Camp Monroe's soldiers relieved the honor guard around the *Saint George,* and immediately set about shielding the monstrous mimic with downed timbers and artificial greenery; a group of seamstresses also sewed camouflaged textiles, and they employed these to great effect. It wasn't perfect, but it was better than leaving their greatest weapon out in the open where it could be seen from the air. Everyone breathed a little easier once the *George* was safe.

As Camp Liberty meshed with Camp Monroe, assignments made their way down the ranks. Calvin dutifully obeyed Hank's order to set up the Rebel Hearts' mimics in the motor pool for inventory purposes, and then he made himself scarce. The prospect of facing Tyler and Hamilton caused him no shortage of fear, even though they still hadn't sent for him.

Survivors poured into the new camp all day, each one inspected and, if necessary, interrogated to confirm their identities. Nobody was allowed within two miles of Camp Monroe without first consuming a spoonful of frosted iron grit, meant to break any concealment charms or potions that would otherwise disguise a wizard spy. When a proper census had been taken and the most pressing matters were under control, the dreaded moment arrived. A pair of guards came to Hank with an arrest order for TechMan Calvin Adler.

Ingvar, Adam, and Emma had all looked to Hank. The brigade leader gave Calvin an almost accusing look, as if to say, *What do you expect?* And Calvin knew the answer. He stepped forward, hands out, before anyone could say anything.

The guards clapped his wrists and ankles in irons, searched him for weapons, and prodded him to get moving. He guessed that they hadn't been told what he'd done, or else they'd have handled him much worse.

"I'm sorry," Calvin said, watching Hank. The guards took Calvin away. "To all of you."

His fellow brigadiers had no reply.

The guards marched him to the disguised *Saint George*, accompanied him up an elevator, and pushed him along a corridor that led to the bridge. Calvin guessed they might be in the dragon's neck, somewhere near the top, but it was hard to keep his bearings while inside. Adjacent to the bridge was a small enclosure with a sliding door, marked as an officer's ready room. Calvin held his face still, though his hands trembled.

One of the guards knocked. Major Tyler bade them enter. They all pushed inside and closed the door behind them, making Calvin all too aware of how small a space it was. The palpable silence fed Calvin's hammering heart; he didn't like being locked in a small room with this woman, bound in shackles, knowing what she must be feeling.

There was a desk between them. On it were a few things he'd seen in her office at Camp Liberty—what little could be salvaged before the dragon machine surfaced and made a royal mess of the base. Her dress uniform's coat hung on the back of her chair. She leaned against the desk in a simple white tank top, her face streaked with soot, wisps of hair having pulled free from her pony tail. A spread of documents and maps held her attention.

"Major? We found TechMan Adler," said one of the guards.

Major Tyler looked up. Her face was impassive, but Calvin knew deep anger when he saw it. Unblinking, unwavering, she said, "Leave him. And fetch Hamilton."

The guards kicked the backs of Calvin's knees. He landed hard on his shins and bit back a grimace as the guards made him cross his ankles and sit atop them. Then they re-cuffed his hands behind his back; he wasn't going anywhere. The guards shuffled out, leaving him with Major Tyler, who exuded the aura of a volcano about to explode.

"I'm keen to stand you in front of this machine and fire everything we've got at you until you're nothing but a pink cloud," the Major seethed. "And the *only* reason I don't is because we used too much ammo securing our escape."

"Then it's a little late to say that I want out," Calvin said. He didn't blink, but his lip quivered.

Major Tyler stepped around the desk and lashed out with her

foot. The kick landed with stunning accuracy, her heel driving straight against his throat. Calvin thought for sure that his windpipe had cracked; talking became impossible, and breathing was not to be taken for granted. He collapsed onto his side, and Major Tyler grabbed his shirt with both hands. Despite their near equal height, and his weight advantage, she yanked him to his feet and shoved him into the door with alarming strength.

"Do you see this?" Tyler snarled, yanking the hem of her tank top out of her trousers. A hideous scar spanned the width of her belly beneath her navel. "I got this from a crude medical practice called *surgery*. Usually it's reserved for sick cattle when they are in labor and the calf is in full breech. They cut you open and pull out damaged parts because your body has no other recourse for survival. Do you know what they cut out of me, Adler? *My daughter.*

"Twelve years ago this spring, my husband and I were expecting our first child. We lived and worked at a bestiary, mucking stalls for the mages. I was eight months pregnant. One day a mage came in, fully inebriated, and began fooling around with an ornery boggart. The boggart gutted him before we could restrain it, and the mage needed serious blood magic to save himself. So he pointed his wand at my husband, who stood at my side, and uttered a foul curse meant to steal the life force from us.

"Only my husband died, and I didn't. In his drunken stupor, the mage stole from my child and left her dead inside my womb. Amateur surgeons removed her from me to save my own life. That is why I joined this army, and that is why I would sell my own soul to wipe the wizard scourge off the face of the land. I tell you that there is nothing in any realm of existence that is more disgusting to me than the mage class.

"Until you came along."

Calvin couldn't rub at his aching throat. He tried to swallow but it made his vision swim. He pushed back against the door, hacking and drooling, wishing against all reason that the pain would stop.

"Years of preparation, wasted! Our entire battle schedule, foiled! Our greatest weapon revealed far too soon! The revolution might be beyond saving. I . . . I don't even know what else to say. You are worth less to me than the ashes of Camp Liberty. I should bury you face down in a latrine but we haven't been here long enough for one to be sufficiently full," Tyler spat.

Calvin choked down a precious gasp of air. "You loved your husband," he rasped.

"Don't you dare talk about him!"

"My parents love each other. They were lucky that way, when the Crown shipped them here to be cheap labor because they didn't have magic." Calvin's throat thickened and he took a few breaths to ease the pain. "I thought we were fighting to change that system, until McCracken sent me here to die because his daughter likes me." Steeling himself, he went all in: "You're fighting McCracken's war and nothing will change even if we win. *Tell me who's no better than the mages?*"

Tyler's gaze could've melted steel. She seized his neck in one hand and squeezed hard enough to turn his vision red. His throat hurt so severely that his legs gave out. Tyler stiff-armed him back to the ground, where he lay in a heap as he tried to breathe.

The door opened and Captain Hamilton announced his arrival. His coat was stained with blood on the back, and through a gash in the fabric Calvin saw bloodied bandages. Hamilton leered down at Calvin with wicked intent in his eyes; payback was coming.

"Major?"

Tyler didn't take her eyes off Calvin. "What, Captain?"

"I found this in the wreckage. It must have come out of the contraband lockers. I know it's a banned item, but given the circumstances, I thought . . ."

The paralyzing ache in his throat kept Calvin from craning his neck to see what Hamilton had. Whatever it was, Tyler was interested. She reached into Hamilton's box and withdrew a circular object, about as wide as the mouth of a teacup, with a dial in the center. Two long metal spikes dangled from steel wires on the bottom, and jagged saw-like teeth ran around the edge of the circular dial. Though Calvin couldn't tell what it was, it looked *evil*. Something told him that Hamilton hadn't "salvaged" this thing at all—this was deliberate.

"What are you suggesting, Captain?" Tyler asked.

"Right now we need to communicate with our other outposts, Major. Since radios are a hazard, we can send messengers."

"We can't spare anyone."

"Ah, but I believe TechMan Adler is willing to atone for his atrocious indiscretion." Hamilton grinned again.

"I'm done helping you," Calvin seethed.

Tyler ignored him. She nodded her consent to Hamilton, replacing the device in his box.

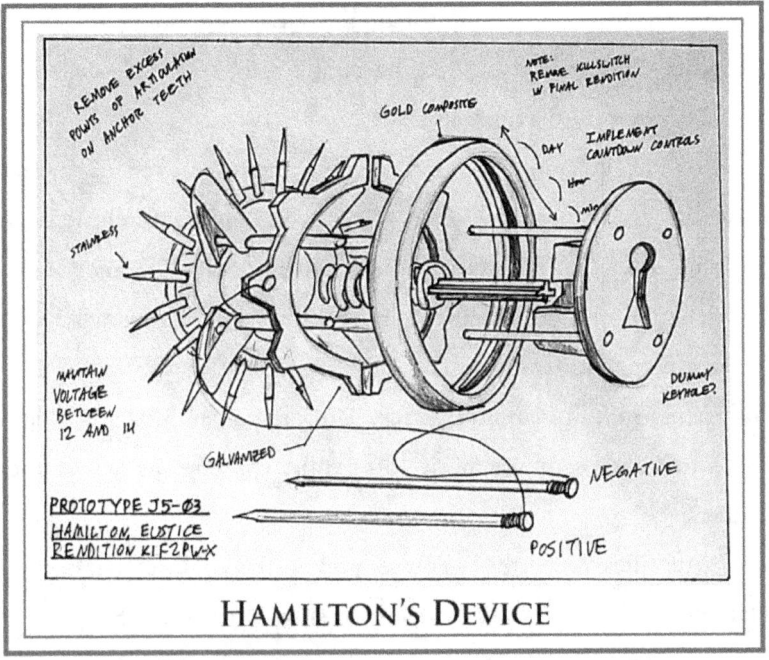

HAMILTON'S DEVICE

"Oh, you're not done yet," Hamilton said, leering at Calvin.

"Be quick and keep it quiet," Major Tyler told him.

"Aye, Major." Hamilton tugged a black cloth hood out of his back pocket, and with one deft hand he wrapped it tight around Calvin's head. Calvin squirmed and shouted, earning him a sharp jab to the skull from someone's knee.

"Weech, Irwin, fetch this scum and take him to sick bay."

Two pairs of hands lifted him off the floor. How far they dragged him, Calvin couldn't tell, though they remained on the

Saint George. Wherever it was that they ended up, they unshackled his hands and slammed him down onto a table. Again he tried to pull free and remove the hood, and again they beat him for it. The guards strapped his arms to the table with thick leather belts, then secured his legs, hips, and torso; the table had no shortage of restraints. When they finished, he couldn't move in the slightest, save to draw very short breaths.

Bright light stung his eyes when Hamilton yanked the hood from his head, running a final strap over Calvin's forehead and cinching it tight. "It goes without saying that I'll enjoy this. Normally I'd drag it out, but we're short on time so this will have to do. And . . . understand that you *deserve* this, after what you did."

Calvin spat in Hamilton's face. The captain jammed a wooden rod into Calvin's mouth none too gently, splitting his lips at the corners.

"Bite down on this. You're gonna feel a little pressure." Hamilton held up the device that he'd shown to Tyler. "See this? I designed it myself. The Major thought it was a little, well, *too much*, but fortunately your bungle made her a little more liberal in the ethics department. This is a timer, you see? But it has no power source, no batteries or clockwork. Instead it draws electricity from the human heart, which provides *just enough* to keep it ticking. That's where these come in."

He held up the two metal spikes—long nails, really—and used them to trace tiny lines down Calvin's chest. The metal felt hot against his skin, which had gone cold and clammy and bright white.

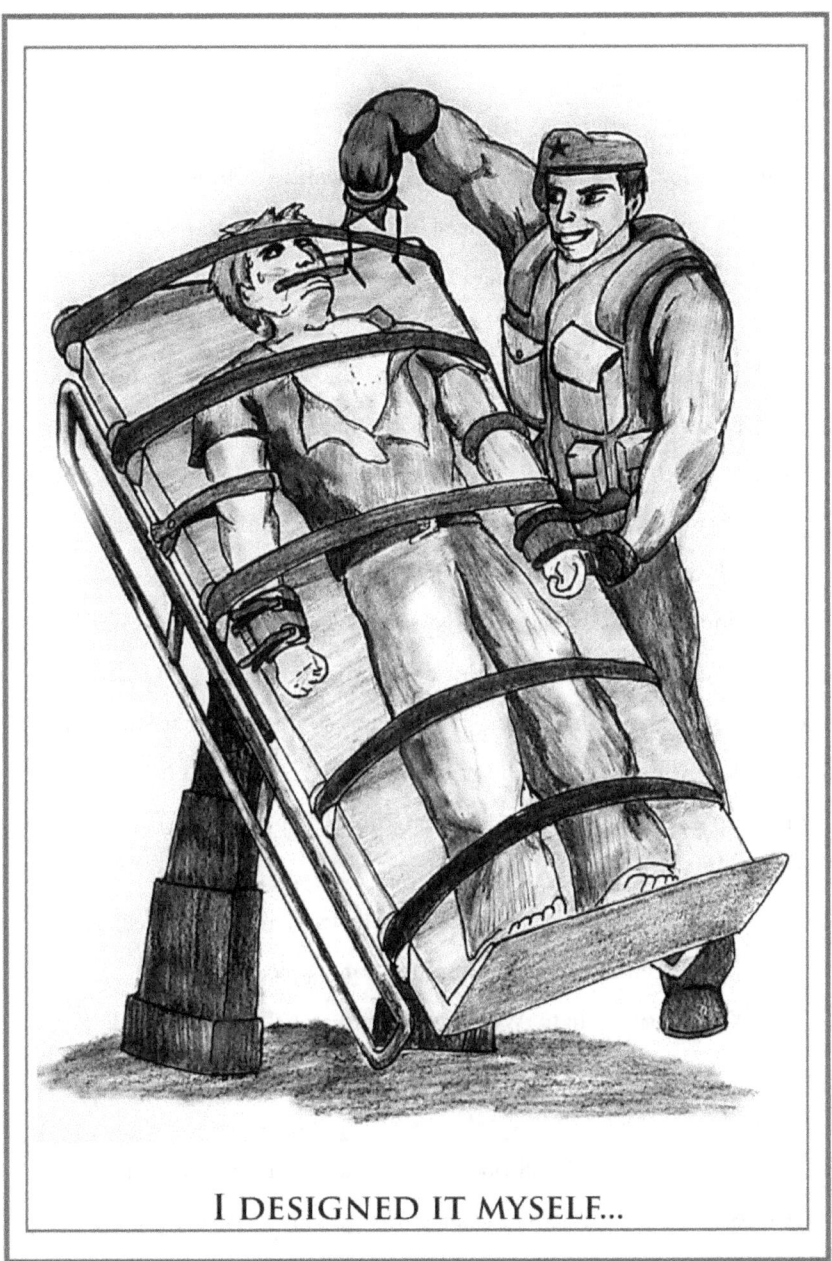

I DESIGNED IT MYSELF...

Was that from the tight straps? Or was it fear?

He knew the answer.

"Aim is everything. I had to practice on half a dozen wizard captives before I got this right." Hamilton's breath stank of tobacco juice and bad hygiene. He slowly twisted one of the nails until it broke the skin; he made a show of frowning at the location, and moved the nail somewhere else. Calvin's guts burned even as his skin grew colder. His head swam, dizzy with anticipation. He tried to spit the rod out and say something, anything, to plead for mercy, but the strap high on his chest kept the necessary muscles from being able to move. Even so, an involuntary whimper escaped his throat.

"There we go! That's the spirit," Hamilton said. He pressed two fingers against the left side of Calvin's sternum. "I've found it's easier to hit a moving target. There's just so much soft tissue in the way, the movement actually makes it *visible* to me, you know?" He lined up the nail again and hesitated, holding it there for several seconds.

Stop! Calvin wanted to scream. He tried to break free, really tried, but the table had been designed for this.

"You know what? We have some anesthetics. Painkillers—they'd numb you up good and proper. Eh, you're tough. I think we can just . . ."

Mid-sentence, Hamilton abruptly thrust his palm against the head of the nail and drove it deep into Calvin's chest, a hair to the left of his breastbone. Calvin felt every microscopic fraction of the steel stabbing through skin and muscle until it reached his heart, resting against the soft organ where it would somehow draw power. Thrashing against the pain, his spine contorted and tightened, every muscle in his body resisting the assault, helpless to save him.

STOP! YOU BASTARD, STOP!

"Wow, first try, all the way in! Guess I'm good at this. Don't worry, only one more of those." Hamilton poked around farther to the left of Calvin's chest, halfway down his side. Calvin heaved and thrashed but still couldn't budge. The strips bit into his skin, and his joints popped with the effort. Was he bleeding? Maybe. All feeling was gone from his extremities. Again he tried to dislodge the stick in his mouth, and failed. Hamilton rammed the second spike between Calvin's ribs with all his strength. Tears gushed out Calvin's eyes and a sharp stink filled the room as he soiled himself.

"Whoa!" Hamilton pinched his nose. "Maybe you're not *that* tough. Let's see, I swear I'm forgetting something. Oops! Here it is."

Razor-sharp teeth slashed against Calvin's left pectoral, and Hamilton leaned into the device with his full weight until the whole thing sat flush on Calvin's skin. He cranked the dial to the right, causing the teeth to flair out and spike upward, hooking his flesh tightly from the underside.

Calvin shrieked. He bit the wood so hard that it snapped. Whether he bit his tongue or his cheek or his lip, he couldn't tell, only that blood gushed from his mouth. The world appeared to drown in a haze of red, threatening his consciousness. He felt Hamilton's foul breath blowing warmly onto his ear.

"I'll tell you a secret, kid: you're not going to survive this device, and I actually regret that. I almost wish you could be present on my wedding day. Alas, I'll just have to settle for a quiet life with my Amelia after the war. Take that thought with you into the wild?" He opened a cap on the face of the dial and pressed a hidden button beneath. Cold fire punched into Calvin's heart, expelling sweat from every pore on his body as the device powered on.

In that moment, Calvin knew what death felt like.

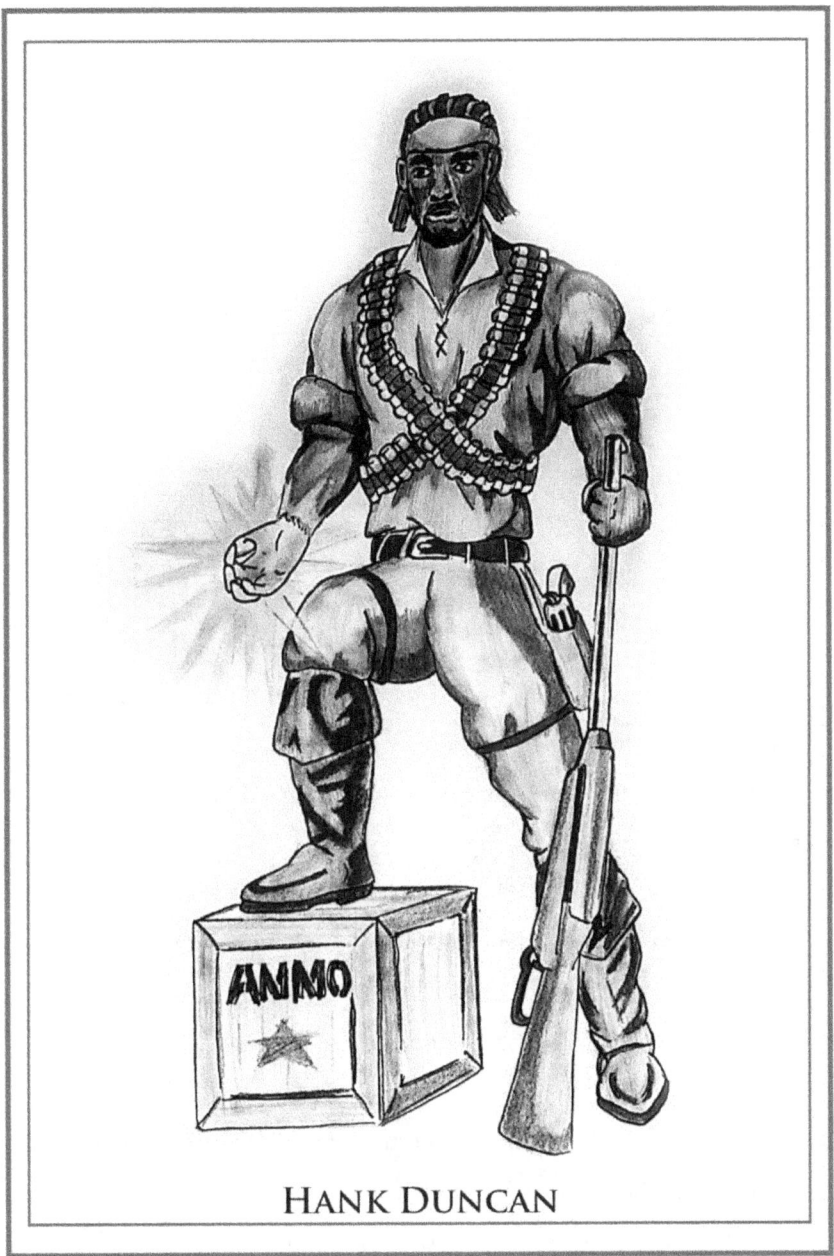

HANK DUNCAN

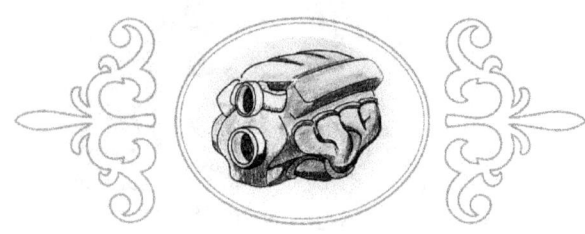

CHAPTER 9

"What's this called? It's just wires hooked up to a dial. Some gears . . . what's it for?"

Rusty took the dial from Stitch's outstretched hand and turned it over.

"It's a speedometer," she said.

"Thought those had needles and numbers on the face and stuff."

"This is what they look like on the inside." She handed it back to him.

"You remember things better than me." Stitch wrapped the wires around the dial and tied it with a string.

"Nah, I pulled one out of this thing yesterday," Rusty muttered. She kicked the broken dragonling that she'd been dismantling. Two months ago a mage had killed the pilot mid-flight, and the salvage crews had recovered the mimic. The body and wings were ruined beyond repair, but the innards were useful.

Stitch sighed and dropped the speedometer into a bucket with the other dashboard components off an outdated warg mimic. Then he went back to attacking the wreck with his wrench, removing whatever would come off without too much hassle. Rusty worked opposite him in the junk shop. Theirs was an easy task, remedial even, which was why the young recruits had to do it. All of the older, "more capable" technomancers were in real brigades right now.

"Stuff this," Rusty said as she sorted copper wiring from steel throttle cables. "This is the most pointless thing we could be doing."

Stitch had nothing comforting to say to that; it was a complaint he'd heard a dozen times since they'd been sent to Trenton, New Jersey. Taking a break to wipe his brow and get a drink of water, Stitch watched the other salvagers working at stuck bolts, armor plating, and engine parts. The foreman went from bench to bench, answering questions and making sure that the untested cadets weren't damaging good bits in the process.

"Something's gotta give soon, Rusty," he said by way of encouragement. "Didn't McCracken say that when we started? It's the twenty-sixth of October. There's supposed to be a big battle in November, that's why we were training so fast."

"Pah. Like they'll include us? They need this junk so they can fix more mimics." Rusty dropped her wrench and slammed a fist on the worktable. "We went through all that training for combat, not housekeeping!"

Nervous, Stitch shushed her. Over the noise of work and chatter, nobody seemed to have heard her. "Keep it down! What if we get in trouble?"

Rusty sighed and sorted the wires again. "Calvin wasn't afraid to get in trouble. They put him on a mimic in the middle of the night and sent him off alone. Lucky."

I'D RATHER BE FIGHTING...

"Well, Calvin was a good flier. And . . . are you saying you'd rather be alone?" The thought made Stitch's heart twinge in a way he hadn't expected; he'd had siblings back when his family worked for Rusty's, and they'd all perished in the raid. Hers too. For survival's sake he'd become her big brother; now the thought of

Rusty out on her own troubled him. He didn't doubt her abilities, but that didn't mean he wanted her too far for him to watch her back.

"I'm saying I'd rather fight mages. We could make a gryphon out of all this junk and go together," Rusty thought aloud.

Stitch couldn't be sure whether or not she was joking. "Where would we go?"

Rusty didn't answer.

Sighing, Stitch took up his wrench and got back to work.

*

"Where'd you learn Spanish?" Cohen asked.

Avery shrugged one shoulder, eyes fixed ahead. "Lived down south for a while, picked it up in Florida. Family traded with Spaniards for years before they died." He tended not to say much on that subject.

The two of them moved stealthily through the smothering brush, careful to remain in sight of their traveling party. When Cohen and Avery had gotten their dispatch from Commodore McCracken, they'd been surprised at how close it was, especially considering where everyone else had gone. They'd learned from their new commanding officer, Major Yahola, that their familiarity with the Spanish language had been the deciding factor.

"Welcome to Camp Winchester," Yahola had said. "Practice your interpersonal skills. The two of you are our newest diplomats."

Cohen and Avery had been equally confused, even after the

briefing. It hadn't made sense until that very morning when they were assigned to go on a long-range mission with some more-experienced diplomats to talk to a settlement of Spanish technomancers in the Georgia province. The TechMan army didn't have any bases that far south, but they did have a loose alliance with Spanish colonials who had fled Florida to get away from their own evil magical monarch. They were excellent craftsmen and had taken to tinkering once they were far enough from *los magos del rey*.

Now the *técnomagos* made weapons and launched stealth attacks against magicians of all nations. Camp Winchester had refurbished some engines for their *coches de guerra* in exchange for the Spaniards making an appearance at a future military strike.

Cohen and Avery kept walking, ever careful to minimize the evidence of their presence in the woods. Avery was good at that; he'd been a forest hermit for a long time before John Penn had found him. Cohen wasn't so careful, though. He tried too hard. Avery thought he was actually quieter when he was distracted.

"What about you? Where'd you learn *la lengua*?" Avery said in a low tone.

Cohen didn't answer. Avery wondered whether he'd heard him. He started to repeat the question, but Cohen spoke up.

"My family is all Spanish Jews. Parents used to live there, little town on the coast, called Gandia. They came here before I was born, but they still taught me the language," he said.

Avery paused and craned his neck to see Cohen's face. "I hear it's not popular to be Jewish in Spain."

"Ain't popular in most of Europe. Or a lot of places here, either."

The way he said it made it clear that there was a story. The fact that he was an orphan meant Avery didn't need to ask about it.

WIN THE WAR, THEN MAKE IT PERSONAL.

"Sorry to hear that," he said, picking up the trail again. The others had gotten ahead; they needed to close the gap.

"We've all lost people. Ain't any harder for me than it is for everyone else," Cohen said.

"You don't believe that."

"I should, for now. Win the war for everybody, then I can make it personal."

Avery nodded. "I like that. You're all right, Cohen."

113

The two of them caught up to the rest of their party and waited for the Spaniards to come.

*

"We can't stay here," Major Tyler said. "We're a drain on your resources and we're too numerous. They'll find us if we don't keep moving."

Major Fox Glenshaw studied a map on his desk, frowning at Major Tyler's proposed course, as well as her limited roster of soldiers.

"It won't make any sense for you to go with just the Liberty outfit. You've taken too many losses, Sam. We can patch the gaps in your ranks, but then we'll be shorthanded. And if we try to take both camps, it'll be easier to spot us," Glenshaw said.

"All we need is make it to H-burg." Tyler tapped the map, marking Harrisburg. "We'll send scout parties ahead, travel at night, and we won't cut any timber."

"You want to go through Bedford?"

"No, we'll go through Altoona."

"That's two hundred miles of wilderness. There's no road."

"So there's barely anyone to cross our path. We can make fifty miles per day, integrate new forces at H-burg, and wait for McCracken's orders. I will need some of your pilots for my mimics," Tyler said.

Glenshaw ran a hand down his jaw. "Damn this whole mess. Right then, let's hop to it." He fished through some documents and handed her a register of unassigned cadets. "Fill your brigades with these. Some of them are fresh out of Mount Vernon, but it's the best I can do."

"It's good enough. Thank you, Fox." Tyler took the list and left Glenshaw's office. Captain Hamilton awaited her outside.

"Orders, Major?" He fell into step beside her. Tyler handed him the list.

"These are our available assets. Get them assigned and get us mobile, Captain. We're legs up by this time tomorrow. And for the love of all that's holy, put someone in 7MB who's got a lick of sense!"

"Aye, Major."

*

Adam topped off the fuel in his gryphon, capped the tank, and thanked the technician for bringing the kerosene cart. The mimic needed some fine-tuning as well, but he was beyond tired. It could wait. Spreading his arms wide as he yawned, he put his tools away and looked for a spot to lie down; Ingvar had taken a prime spot under their gryphon's wing, also exhausted from the long and sudden trek. Emma lay curled up a few feet away, though one arm was stretched toward the Techno Viking, her fingers probing for him in her sleep. Adam smirked; he'd long suspected they were sweet on each other. It just needed time.

As he rolled out his sleeping mat, a wave of chatter bubbled through ranks of soldiers around them, growing louder as it drew near; Captain Hamilton was headed their way with a company of unfamiliar faces at his back, pointing and issuing orders as he went.

Some of these fresh-faced technomancers broke off and introduced themselves to the different brigades, setting their rucksacks with those of their new comrades.

Beefing up the ranks, Adam thought to himself. He'd been expecting this.

When the procession reached 7MB, Hamilton raised his eyes to the Rebel Hearts' flag, hanging from the spoiler on Adam's mimic. He didn't need to be a mind reader to know what Hamilton was thinking.

"Where's your commanding officer, TechMan Paige?"

"Indisposed, sir," Adam said. "I'll accept the newcomers."

"Won't be necessary," said a voice behind Adam. Hank appeared, trudging in from the treeline, looking better than he had in days. "What's the haps, Cap?"

Hamilton ignored the lack of decorum, too tired to make an issue of it. "Changes to your roster. You're getting two rookies and a third gryphon. Ready 'em quick, 'cause we leave tomorrow." He signaled for the new recruits, a teen boy and a girl about the same age. They dropped their rucks behind Hank's mimic.

"Aye, Captain," Hank said, bored.

Hamilton left. The boy walked right up to Hank, all manners and class, looking more chipper than he had a right to. He'd probably come from money.

"Edsel Winford, sir. Pilot in training!"

"You don't have to 'sir' me, Edsel, I'm just a brigade leader. Call me Hank. This is Adam, that's Ingvar, that's Emma. And you

REPORTING FOR DUTY!

are?" Hank looked to the girl, who was nothing if not easy on the eyes.

"Lyla Ecclestone. I'm mostly a gunner ." She stepped past Edsel and stuck out her hand.

Her *right* hand.

Hank smiled and shook it. Adam tensed, unable to peel his

eyes from Hank's wrist. *It's all right, it's all right . . . he was careful. Nobody knows.*

There weren't many technomancers outside of the Rebel Hearts who would accept a fellow soldier that could do magic.

Lyla arched an eyebrow and pulled her hand back, studying her palm, which had a fine layer of damp soil on it.

"Oh, sorry about that," Hank said, brushing his hand against his pants. Adam couldn't help noticing that it looked a little too . . . unmarred, compared to the other. He'd have to disguise it better. "We haven't had time to clean up since we got here."

"All good," Lyla said. Edsel gave her a handkerchief to use.

Yup. Money kid, Adam noted.

"So! When do we get to fly?" Edsel asked, bobbing on the balls of his feet.

"Too soon, kid. Let's check out your mimic." Hank flexed the fingers of his right hand as he walked away, leading the cadets to a new machine.

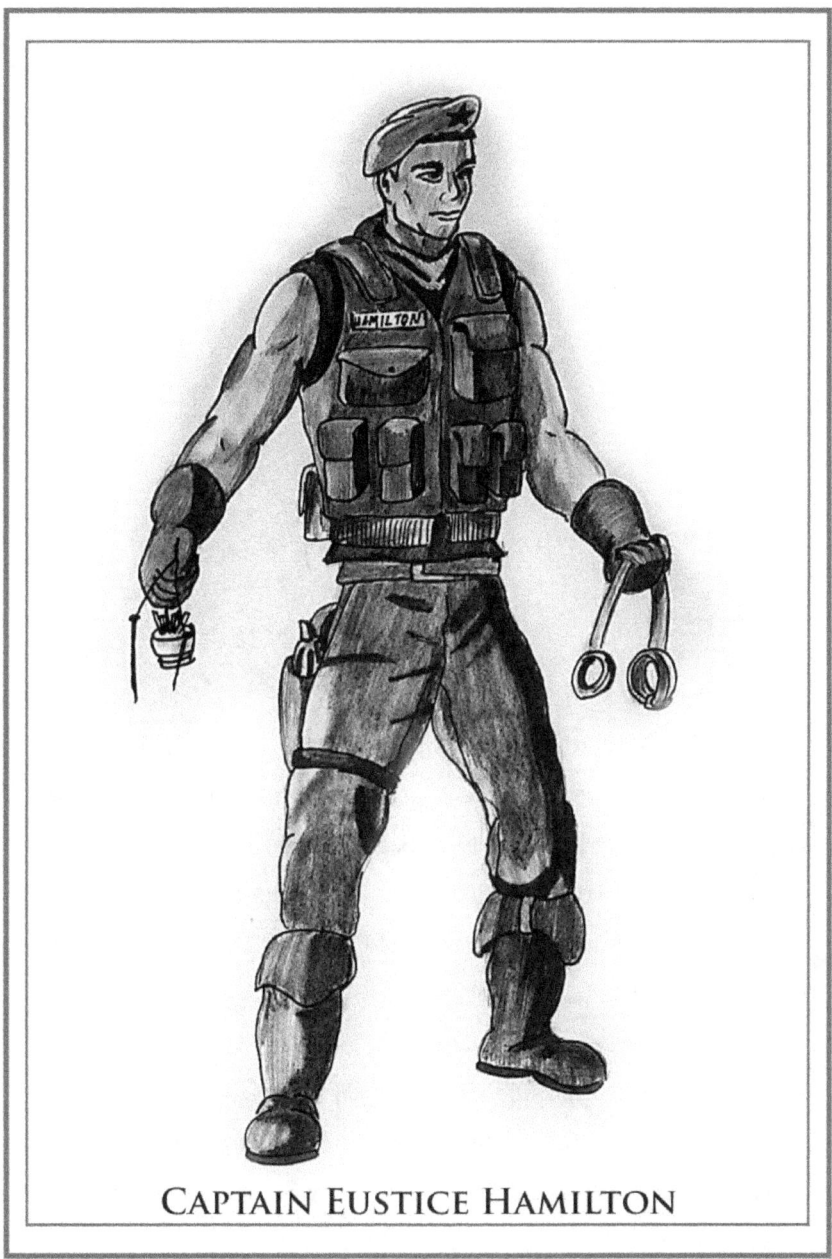

CAPTAIN EUSTICE HAMILTON

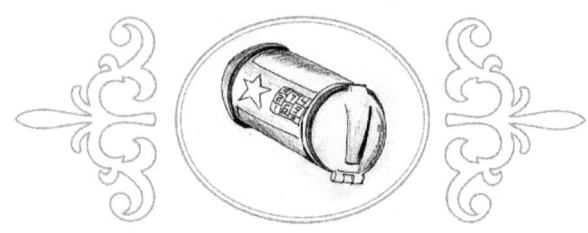

CHAPTER 10

"Adler. *Adler?*"

Hamilton's words pushed through thick fog in Calvin's ears, but he didn't move until the captain smacked him hard on the cheek. The sting brought him back to consciousness and he swatted back at Hamilton, then cried out at the biting pain in his chest. He curled up on the hard, cold ground, holding his breath until the sensation faded.

So it *hadn't* been a nightmare.

"We're here, you clod." Hamilton grabbed Calvin's torn, bloody shirt, and dragged him to his feet. He may have been a sorry excuse for a man, but Hamilton was undeniably strong. Calvin found his legs and held himself up, saying nothing; the sting in his chest occupied his full attention. Unable to raise his throbbing head, he stared in disbelief at deep purple and green bruises surrounding the device. His wrists were severely chafed where the handcuffs had bitten into them, and then there was the time that he'd introduced his face to the ground behind a bench. Everything hurt.

Forcing his eyes open, Calvin blinked away the bright morning sunlight and saw that they were outside. The humming sensation against his bare feet told him two things: he was aboard a mimic, and they'd taken his shoes.

It was a gryphon mimic, hovering off the ground in an unfamiliar wood. A second gryphon hovered nearby, and both the gunner and the pilot had weapons trained on him. So did Hamilton and the pilot of their gryphon.

"What . . ." Calvin croaked. His throat, dry as paper, produced no other sound.

"Brace yourself." Hamilton shoved him. Calvin grunted and tumbled off the back of the gryphon, windmilling his arms all the way down. He landed hard on the damp ground. Clenching his teeth and sucking in breaths against a new wave of pain, he looked up and saw that the four guns were still on him.

"Wait!" He managed to say, holding up a hand to stop them.

"We're not gonna execute you, you twit. Jeez, they must grow 'em real stupid in Baltimore." Hamilton rolled his eyes. "You've got a mission."

"Where am I?" Calvin demanded, wanting to ask a hundred other questions, all of which would've made him sound weak, pathetic, scared, and he wouldn't give Hamilton the satisfaction. The guy was all smiles, like he'd just won the war.

"Ten miles east of Pittsburgh. You're welcome! We just gave you a head start. You get to carry a message the rest of the way," Hamilton said.

"Message?"

A frosted iron canister struck him in the side of the head, thrown by one of the other technomancers. It was thin and light, but it still stung. Calvin let out an involuntary whimper and rubbed his skull.

"It's all in there. Captain Epps will know what to do with it—he's at Trenton. Oh, and I'd hustle, Adler. The clock's ticking, and you're three hundred miles off target." Hamilton tapped his own chest with a wry smile.

"Trenton? Where is Trenton?" Calvin shouted, but the pilots revved their engines and sped off. Hamilton waved good-bye, cackling as they disappeared into the high brush. The engines faded, and Calvin found himself alone in a wilderness he didn't know, pressed in on all sides by trees and bugs and beasts and unfriendly tribes, and he couldn't hold it in any longer. He fell to his knees and sobbed like he hadn't since he was a child.

Damn that Eustice Hamilton and the evil that birthed him. Damn Major Tyler for propping him up, damn John Penn for recruiting in Baltimore, and damn Godfrey Norrington for surviving Calvin's grenade in the woods that night. Furious, Calvin snatched up the iron canister and broke it open against a rock. It

THE CLOCK'S TICKING...

contained a single sheet with tight, handwritten text so fine he had to squint to read it.

CALVIN ADLER, NO RANK, REPORTING FOR SALVAGE DUTY.

As if he'd ever deliver another message like that.

Disgusted, Calvin threw it aside. Damn the technomancers. Hadn't Adam or Hank been talking about "fair trials" after the war? Something called *habeas corpus* and "due process" and the like, saying anyone charged of a crime would have a fair chance to defend himself before being sentenced? It was a luxury they didn't enjoy under King Charles.

Well, they were fooling themselves if they thought that the leadership would just give that kind of power to the people. Damn Tyler and Hamilton and all the rest of them! Even if they won, nothing would change.

He curled up into a ball and felt sorry for himself all the way until sundown, his mind drifting in and out of consciousness. When his breathing finally quieted in his own ears, he noticed the ticking sound from under his shirt.

The clock's ticking.

Calvin pulled his shirt open and pressed his chin to his chest, trying to read the figures on the dial in the fading light. It had three rings in it, each of them numbered. The outermost represented minutes; the next one was hours, and the smallest one in the center represented days.

Nine days, fourteen hours, thirty-seven minutes. *Tick, tick, tick.*

He let a minute go by until the outermost dial rotated to thirty-six. So it was a countdown. That was how much time Calvin had until . . . what? He didn't know. If Hamilton had designed this thing, it could only mean pain or death, probably both. Calvin had to get it out. It would hurt, but he was no stranger to pain any more.

"Done with this." He picked at the head of one nail until it was off his skin, then hooked his fingertips under the edge and gave it a gentle tug.

He regretted it.

"ACK!"

A shock of deep pain struck him in the heart, and he smelled smoke. The dial on the device ticked more rapidly, the minute-marker moving twice as fast.

Tick-tick-tick-tick-tick!

Cursing, Calvin tried to shove the nail back down. Another, more brutal shock to the heart knocked him out cold.

*

Night was in full swing when he awoke this time. His thumb rested over the head of the nail—had he pushed it back in? He couldn't remember, but he must have; the ticking had resumed its old cadence. Maybe he could turn the dials back? No, Hamilton had pushed a button after setting the dials. It wouldn't be beaten so easily, and he didn't dare try to cheat it again. Stopping it was out of the question. The device was there to stay.

One thing was for sure: he wouldn't waste his time in Trenton.

Let Tyler use the damned radio if she wanted to talk to them. Calvin wished to stay far away from the technomancers, but that presented a problem: who else could remove Hamilton's device? He didn't like the prospect of death at fifteen.

Yet if he was really facing the last nine days he would ever have, well, as sick as it made him feel, he knew how he wanted to use the time. A small part of him considered returning to Baltimore, but Mother and Father had at least gotten some closure, to say nothing of the gold. On the other hand, what did Amelia think of his departure? What lies had McCracken told her? Was she wondering what happened to him? Did she know that Hamilton thought she was his betrothed? Was it . . . was it wrong to tell her that he loved her?

He ached to see her again. On top of that, she was smart; maybe she could beat this thing.

There were so many reasons to go to her. He only cared about one. Even if she couldn't save him, if she at least knew the truth, she could flee, and live her own life. She would be safe from Hamilton. That was something.

Broken, battered, exhausted beyond anything he'd endured before, Calvin took a minute to find some stars in the waning light and set his course. He walked, hoping the movement would warm his chilled muscles.

Before long, he started to run.

*

Like never before, numbers spun through his head, even when

his thoughts wandered.

He remembered that he knew of a town called Trenton. It was north of Baltimore, in Jersey. Calvin and his father had spent one night there on that trip to Boston when he was a kid. The memory didn't help him, as hadn't a clue how far it was. However, he knew that Pittsburgh was about two hundred and fifty miles away from Baltimore, and that Baltimore was north-northeast of Mount Vernon by about fifty miles.

Three hundred miles to Mount Vernon from Pittsburgh.

Under nine days to get there.

Better make it eight, so he had time to sneak in and find her.

Eight days, three hundred miles . . . thirty-one miles a day. He couldn't run it all straight, but he figured he could run at least five hours and hope he didn't sleep too long the next day. He'd tread carefully when possible, to spare his bare feet any more injury. He'd need food and water. He had no weapons, no time to make any. That meant stealing. Better to steal food than weapons, and save the time hunting.

He calculated for miles, storing the numbers he needed, discarding the rest. His feet thumped the ground over and over, counting, dividing, adjusting when he slowed down and anticipating when he could speed up. *Five thousand, two hundred and eighty feet in a mile. Three feet in a long stride. One thousand, seven hundred and sixty strides will make a mile. Two-oh- five, and six, and seven . . .*

So much of it was guesswork, and yet it kept him sane as he pushed onward. Avoid cities and towns, avoid mages, avoid

TechMans, and keep going.

All his life, he had gone barefoot on the farm well into the cold season so as to preserve his shoes and socks longer. He was glad for that now, but his feet were starting to burn. Phantom bites warned of blisters to come, and deeper aches threatened his bones, but he didn't stop.

His life. His terms.

Save Amelia. Shaft Hamilton. Make McCracken bleed.

Only Calvin could decide when he was done.

He kept running.

KARAHKWA

CHAPTER 11

Two days.

After two days, he wanted to kill himself. Just yank out the nails and pull on the device until it . . . well, whatever it did that would finish him off.

Maybe he was being weak. He just had to bite down and push harder, everything would be fine. It had only been two days!

Ugh. Two days. An eternity of running as hard as he could for as long as he could, prodding himself back to a trot when his legs begged for a brief stride. Nothing in life was worth this. Nothing was stronger than the constant, growing, never-ending pain.

Don't forget about her.

It was his desire, his *need* to see Amelia that dragged him across the terrain, broken and injured and on the brink of death, pulled by her invisible hand.

Thud. Thud. Thud. His heels punched the ground. His shins ached like they'd been struck with hammers. Yesterday he'd ripped off his shirt sleeves and tore them into strips, which he then used to bind the hot, swollen flesh above his ankles to keep it tight against the bone. Along the way he chewed on plants that he recognized from Shantewa Goodall's botany lessons, for what little relief they offered. It was minor, but it was something.

His breath grated out through his dry throat, and his lips cracked. When he found a river that flowed east, he tried to swim in it. The necessary strokes required too much upper body movement, which tugged at the hooks in his chest. For good or evil, water didn't seem to affect the device's function, so he floated on his back, resting, letting the current do the work, until he dozed off and nearly drowned. Soon the current slowed and the temperature did him more harm than good, and when he climbed out to start running again he thought his cold legs might shatter.

The chill was a new pest to deal with, but at least his leg pains had eased.

He ran. He walked. He crawled when he could do nothing else. He slept only when his body shut down, when his will could no longer dominate his flesh.

Two days. For the first time in his life, he had an idea of what it was to be truly broken. He wasn't there yet . . .

. . . but he was close.

On the third day, he woke before the autumn sun, shivering in the remains of his camp fatigues. Winter was close and he was beyond unprepared; people died in conditions less drastic than these. Some part of him thought that didn't sound so bad.

No! Stop being weak.

A quarter-moon hung in an ocean of stars across the sky. His fatigued mind began working out constellations, trying to estimate his progress. Even his most generous estimate brought fresh tears to his eyes.

He was not as close as he needed to be.

The sun rose and beckoned him to keep running. He passed a farm by a corn field and helped himself to some of the golden crop, wondering if the juicy kernels had always tasted this sweet, and for a moment he forgot that he was tired and still had so much ground to cover.

Noon came. Fifteen miles down, at least. Still not enough, and yet the best he could do. He pushed through a particularly thick wood, ignoring bites from the bugs that homed in on his stench, leeching off his anguish. With his legs on the verge of shattering, and a tremendous ache in his heart that was more than physical, Calvin fell to his knees, then to all fours, hanging his head in despair.

By the time he noticed he was bawling, he'd been at it for several minutes. A surge of primal desperation boiled up within him and he straightened into a kneeling position, threw his head back and screamed at the sky.

"SOMEBODY! HELP ME!"

He hadn't expected an answer. All the same, he received one.

It was not a voice that used words, but rather a *presence* that touched his mind, igniting a lost sense of hope, need, and promise, such as he hadn't felt in far too long. The sensation proved so powerful that it could only have come from somewhere else, not from within him. He knew he had nothing like this left inside.

What was going on?

Calvin closed his eyes and listened. His heart thumped erratically and the device still *tick-tick-tick*ed along, but there was something more, a scratching sound through the trees to his right. Standing up with the aid of a nearby sapling, Calvin worked his way through the brush for a few yards until it opened up into a man-made clearing. There was a lean-to made of wood and canvas, a fire pit full of dull embers, and stocks of supplies piled neatly off to one side. Several animal furs hung from a wooden rack, carefully left to dry.

And right in the middle of the camp, bound with cords and tied to thick stakes in the ground, was the biggest damn bird he'd ever laid eyes on.

It had to be twenty feet long, with four wings tucked to its sides. The bird lay on its belly, its elegant plume of brilliant red feathers mussed and crumpled, and its beak was held shut by a leather thong. Calvin recalled a drawing from a schoolbook back in Baltimore, depicting this exact kind of creature, calling it a "megafowl." Its common name was 'thunderbird.'

He couldn't believe it. An actual *thunderbird,* a beast of legend that had been hunted near to the brink of extinction, here, trussed

A THUNDERBIRD!

up and alone in the forest.

Calvin looked skyward again, wondering who—or what—had answered his cry for help.

*

Godfrey had had it with brooms. Sod the monitors, he was going to use the teleportal network. He meditated until he could detect the nearest opening—a few hours away on foot—and grumbled to himself the whole way there. Being wand-less and distant from the lodestone caused him to work up a sweat as he focused the necessary magic to open the gate, but at long last, it popped open, like a hole in the air.

He took a circuitous route to Belle Chasse—fixed teleportals drew less attention, after all—and once he was there, he commandeered a horse from a French duffer and rode the rest of the way. When he arrived at Kalfu LeVeau's swamp shack, the old sangromancer was leaning back in a porch chair, smoking a pipe with a mile-wide smile on his face.

"You found him, then?" Kalfu blew smoke rings with no apparent effort.

"Oh, I found him all right. Slippery git got away, and caused me no shortage of trouble in the process!"

"Mmm. And you would not have returned here if you didn't have to."

Pursing his lips, Godfrey pointed at his injured neck, where the metal cuffs had nearly choked him. "Most of this blood is mine, but I'd bet some is his too. You interested?"

"Interested in how he choked you with handcuffs?"

"I never mentioned handcuffs."

"I know." Kalfu's lips spread into a grin as he sucked his pipe.

"Are you sure you're blind?"

"Eyes are not the only window to the world around you, *mon fils*."

"I'm not your son!"

The sangromancer chuckled. "Not yet. Give us a look at that blood." He set the pipe down, took up his staff, and descended the porch steps. Extending a hand to Godfrey's neck, he closed his eyes and hummed to himself, as if he were musing over an interesting find. The man stank of smoke and too many days without a proper bath; Godfrey held his breath until the sangromancer finished, stepping back with a small reddish-brown pellet of dried blood that floated between his hands.

"That's his, then?" Godfrey exhaled. "What do you see?"

"Tais-toi," Kalfu barked. His lips kept moving as he worked on the blood. Godfrey gritted his teeth at the rebuke but held his tongue.

"He is no longer in the Ohio," Kalfu whispered.

"You can track him with that?"

Kalfu seemed not to hear. "Moving slowly. Injured. Tired." The sangromancer arched his eyebrows. "He is in quite a state. Mutilated, but not by magic. His body and spirit are close to breaking, and yet his heart is wild." He licked his lips. "A weaker soul would be dead already. He will not go quietly."

"I gathered that." Godfrey rubbed sourly at his throat.

Kalfu squeezed his eyes tighter, as though he were reading something of great interest printed on the insides of his eyelids. "Can it be . . ." he whispered.

"Now what?"

"You must take me to meet him," Kalfu suddenly said.

"What? No, he's my quarry. I can't go home without him."

"I said I must *meet* him. You can have him when I am through."

"Why?" Godfrey's voice cracked a little.

Kalfu blinked several times and shook his head, ending the magical trance. "I have my reasons. I will help you capture him, and you will give me a few minutes in his presence. This is the payment I demand."

Godfrey thought it over. "Fine. When can we leave?"

"Do not be so hasty, Godfrey Norrington; all the King's witches and all the King's men could not make Calvin's rebel knees bend. We shan't underestimate him; we would do well to enlist another wizard to help us capture him."

"There's something you're not telling me, Kalfu," Godfrey accused.

Again, that smug grin, hiding so much. "Indeed. Yet I repeat myself: if you had another option, you wouldn't come to me."

Much as Godfrey hated it, Kalfu was right. Godfrey paced back and forth, thinking it over. "Fine, we'll get a third. I hope you know someone, 'cause I've nobody to reach out to."

"*Pas de problemme.* I have someone in mind, and he's no one to be trifled with. He fishes alligators for a living."

*

Numbers spun, the device ticked, and everything inside Calvin howled at him to keep moving. Still, he didn't move.

A thunderbird. Right there, wrapped up as pretty as a birthday gift.

It couldn't be true. Nothing this good happened to him lately. He puzzled through it, scratching his head. What would it do if he untied it? Offer him a ride in exchange for the favor? An absurd notion—it was an animal. Majestic, no doubt, but also feral. Gratitude could only be a foreign concept for it.

The bird's eye snapped open and locked on Calvin's face with frightening intensity. Calvin grunted and nearly collapsed as a wave of nausea struck him. The forest spun, and for a moment his thoughts were not his own. His sight went foggy, then dark, then came back into focus in extremely sharp detail, in a spread of vibrant colors he could never describe. He saw . . .

Himself?

The bird blinked. Calvin's sight blinked out too, then refocused. He raised a hand to his forehead and saw himself raising his hand. Sudden hope filled his heart and he tried to flap his wings, only they were pinned down under the ropes.

No, not *his* wings; the bird's wings.

What in the blazes? Was he *in the bird's head?* Calvin was feeling his own feelings, thinking his own thoughts, yet he was definitely

138

feeling and thinking what the bird felt and thought too. As he came to this realization, a sense of calm understanding settled in his brain, as if the bird were nodding its head.

"How?" Calvin asked.

It was just something the bird could do.

"Okay . . ."

The bird had a name: Karahkwa. And he needed help.

"Help with what?"

Karahkwa showed Calvin a day-old memory. The clearing they were in, the fire pit off to the side, the canvas tent . . . inside the tent. Yes, inside there was a chest of small drawers. Bottom drawer. Vials. Blood.

A thought tickled Calvin's mind, some memory from a class at Mount Vernon: certain magic tricks centered on hurting or controlling people by getting samples of their blood. Distance was not a factor with this kind of magic; if someone had your blood, you could be on the moon and they could still hurt you.

Karahkwa had been caught and tied up. His captors had a blood sample. Even if Calvin were to cut him loose, his captors could force him to come back.

Burn it. Calvin could burn Karahkwa's blood. Suddenly the thought of asking for a favor seemed reachable. He patted Karahkwa's wing. Yes! He would do it.

Karahkwa relaxed; a relieved sigh.

"I'll get it." Calvin limped over to the tent, noting other things in the camp that he hadn't at first: stacks of hollow bones, bundles of exotically colored feathers, and about a dozen beaks.

Hunted almost to extinction. Karahkwa had been brought down by trophy hunters. They intended to harvest this creature for his parts, take what they could get, and discard the rest.

Kind of like what the technomancers had done to him.

"I know how you feel," he muttered as he rummaged through the tent. He found the drawer of blood vials exactly where he'd seen it, and he studied their labels. Karahkwa didn't see the one he was looking for until Calvin picked up a larger vial made of light green glass. The bird struggled vigorously against his ropes, blinking over and over again so hard that Calvin had to breathe deep to keep from getting dizzy.

"I've got it! It's here, okay?" He left the tent and went to the campfire. He had just uncorked the vial and was about to dump the blood onto the smoldering coals when the green glass *exploded* in his hand. With a jolt, Calvin dropped the whole thing into the fire pit. A few feet to his left, a tomahawk thudded into the ground.

Footsteps in the woods! Calvin turned his head toward the sound, and this simple act saved his life. An arrow sliced past his ear so close that the tail feathers brushed his cheek. With a scream he dropped down, his muscles howling. Deep in the trees he caught the faintest shadow of a man sprinting through the foliage, almost invisible.

Iroquois, in the woods—they were shooting at him!

Scrambling to recover the tomahawk, Calvin took cover behind Karahkwa. The bird sharpened his focus and saw the plants moving in different spots, indicating more men hiding in the brush. Karahkwa sent Calvin an impulse so intense that it nearly manifested itself as words in his mind.

Cut, he thought.

Trembling, Calvin grabbed one of Karahkwa's restraints and sawed it open with the tomahawk's blade. *Cut faster! Get him free! He can take you to Amelia!*

Karahkwa grunted. An arrow struck his side, but the bird had a tough skin beneath his tight feathers. One rope snapped and Calvin immediately attacked the next one, but there was slack now. He pushed it to the ground with one foot and hacked it apart.

Brush and twigs snapped under heavy footfalls in the woods. A war cry sounded, and an Iroquois man charged into the clearing, arm cocked back to throw a long knife.

Snap! Karahkwa tore the rest of the rope apart with the strength of one wing. All at once his binds unraveled from his body and he spread his limbs wide, catching the Iroquois man on the jaw so hard that he flew backward, struck the tent, and brought it down in a heap.

"Whoa!" Calvin jumped back, landing hard on his rump.

The other men burst from the trees with weapons in hand. Calvin rolled over and over to escape their incoming missiles, which seemed to be coming for both him and Karahkwa.

The bird reared up on its thick, muscular feet and, with one razor-sharp talon, hooked the thong on his beak and sliced it off. Fully liberated, Karahkwa spread his four wings to a span that made the wide clearing look cramped.

The hunters stopped dead in their tracks, brandishing their weapons and shouting to each other in a garbled mix of Iroquois and French. Calvin snuck a peak and was surprised to see two Frenchmen in colonial clothing, working alongside the Iroquois. What were Frenchmen doing this deep into British territory? They looked ragged, like the way Calvin felt. Perhaps they were refugees also, but right now they were hunting Karahkwa, and that made them enemies.

Calvin was just about to throw the tomahawk at them when Karahkwa opened his beak and drew in a deep breath, one that puffed up his chest to nearly twice his size, a feat Calvin would have thought impossible. One of the Iroquois men screamed and nocked an arrow, aiming for Karahkwa's expanded lung; another Iroquois tried to stop him from releasing the string. As they fought, Karahkwa unleashed his most dangerous weapon of all, and Calvin soon realized that the hunters never stood a chance.

The bird shrieked. It was more than that . . . it was a thunderclap, the sound by which his species had earned its name.

A mighty booming *crack* broke the sky apart. Dirt, rocks, flaming embers, all of it exploded in a rushing cloud. The hunters flew, *flew*, with their feet off the ground and everything, back into the woods, engulfed in a wave of debris and sound for which they had not been prepared. Their bodies hurdled into the trees, which also bent under the terrible force of the cry. The sound wave died out almost as fast as it had begun, returning the woods to an eerie, calm silence, save for the ringing in Calvin's ears. At the closest edge of the clearing there remained only bare trunks and the wreckage of the hunters' camp.

Calvin uttered a profanity that he reserved for special occasions. He couldn't even hear the words escape his lips.

Drawing in a second breath, Karahkwa flapped his wings and kicked up more dust. Eyes wide with panic, Calvin jumped up and lunged for a rope that dangled from Karahkwa's ankle. The action made the device tear his chest again, yet he held fast as he was yanked into the sky.

Squeezing his eyes shut, Calvin bit down hard, gasping with the effort of holding on. Karahkwa was fast, much more so than a mimic. His arms burned and his chest bled in protest, but he didn't dare let go—at this height and speed, death was guaranteed. Summoning the last dregs of his will, he pulled himself all the way onto Karahkwa's back, crying as he went.

Karahkwa reached out to Calvin with a feeling akin to gratitude. Tears gave way to a budding sense of hope; for the first time, Calvin dared to think he would make it. He patted Karahkwa's back, then almost immediately slumped forward and drifted to sleep, willing the noble bird to carry him to Amelia.

HAMMOND BIRTWISTLE

CHAPTER 12

Amelia's soft hair brushed Calvin's fingers like the downy fluff of an infant lamb. She drew closer to him until her hair cascaded across his arm, his face, his whole front, and he reveled in the smell of her, feeling more at home, more belonging than he had in ages.

"I thought you weren't coming back," she murmured.

"I've missed you," Calvin said.

Amelia squawked. Loudly. Right in his ear.

"Huh?"

Calvin jolted awake, spitting out a mouthful of Karahkwa's feathers, which flitted away in the fast-moving wind. He reeled at the vivid qualities of the dream, and as it faded, intense heartache gripped him. Not the literal ache of the device, but a deeper anguish at the notion of not seeing Amelia again before the contraption went off.

No! Don't think that way. He'd see her. They'd shut it down together. First things first.

He rubbed sleep from his eyes. Wind whipped at his hair and tunic; they were still airborne, flying fast. The now-familiar projection of Karahkwa's thoughts suggested that they'd covered a tremendous distance, and it was time for them to part ways.

Calvin perked up at this: had Karahkwa pried Mount Vernon's location from his dreams? Where they already there? He couldn't tell. Wherever they were, the air smelled different. Breathing quick against the stiffness in his muscles, he worked his neck to one side and gazed down past Karahkwa's massive bulk; even in the waning light of evening, he could tell that he'd never been over these woods before. The trees were wrong, the ground too rocky, the feeling all too . . . unfamiliar.

"Where are we?"

Karahkwa responded with a wave that knocked Calvin onto his back. Anxiety hammered through him, and his heart ached even worse against the nails in it. This was a sensation that Calvin knew very well, the drive to find someone very important to him. For Karahkwa, it was the *need* to reach his mate.

Ehnita. That was her name. She was still a great distance away, and despite knowing that the hunters no longer had her blood, Karahkwa wouldn't rest until she was again by his side. It was that sense of need that had invaded Calvin's dreams, making them feel all the more real.

Have mercy, Calvin thought as he sat up and rubbed his head. Then he froze: what had Karahkwa said? Calvin had destroyed *her* blood? Hadn't the vial belonged to Karahkwa?

No. Another mental impulse confirmed it: Calvin had misunderstood. The hunters had taken Ehnita's blood, using it as bait to trap Karahkwa. Until Calvin had destroyed it, Karahkwa could never have had any assurance of Ehnita's safety.

Calvin palmed his eyes and tried to convey to Karahkwa that he had a love of his own, and he needed to get to her. He pleaded for several minutes, garnering only curt replies before the thunderbird finally shut him down with a resounding *no*. The problem was their destinations: Amelia was south of them, but Ehnita was west. That was all there was to it.

"I helped you! I saved her!" Calvin screamed into the wind.

Without warning, Karahkwa dived hard and fast toward a curving river down below, like a missile. He twisted abruptly to the side and bucked Calvin out into the open air, his side slapping painfully against the river's surface, reminding him of all the abuse his body had endured of late. He skipped once, then sank like a stone into the shockingly cold water, limbs flailing as he clawed his way back to the top. Sputtering, he struggled over to the eastern shore, cringing at the sting in his chest; two more hooks had torn free on impact, drawing blood.

Quaking and panting on the muddy bank, Calvin watched Karahkwa's silhouette shrink into the sunset. He bellowed every

STRUGGLING TO SHORE...

ugly word that he knew, knowing they wouldn't reach the bird's ears. If only he'd just ignored the stupid flying chicken dinner and let him die; now he had no damned clue where he was.

Night fell. Judging by the stars, he wasn't any closer to Virginia, just further west instead of north. A pox on the cruel luck that had allowed him to hope for relief!

Again the chill had diminished his aches, so he re-tied the fabric around his shins and got to running, gently increasing his cadence over time. He didn't bother charting a strict course, instead aiming south by southeast, his thoughts centered only on how little time remained to reach Amelia. According to the numbered dials in his chest, he'd been moving for four days.

No more distractions. No more helping others. There was only the run.

*

Another two days passed. He made fewer calculations now, caring only for the immediate needs of rest and nourishment when he could manage it. If he crossed farmland, he stole from the storehouses. If he was close enough to the barn, he grabbed other provisions; he replaced his tattered, blood-stained shirt and found a pair of boots that were only slightly too large, a problem he remedied with a pair of gloriously thick socks. And he got back to running.

He wouldn't call it luck that he found these things. Calvin was bereft of luck. This was just chance.

Mid-afternoon the next day—three and a half days to go, and

counting—his stomach growled and his legs begged him to stop. He had new blisters on his feet, a result of adjusting to the boots, but at least the cuts on his soles were healing up. He allowed himself his first real respite since falling off of Karahkwa, and before long he came across yet another unexpected boon: the unmistakable aroma of meat smoking over an open flame. His stomach rumbled again, and his nose practically dragged him to the scent.

He followed his nose to a vacant camp in the woods, some hundred yards off the main road. Someone had left the fire going, and over that fire a whole pork shoulder crackled and roasted, leaking fatty juices into the coals, filling the air with sweet, smoky goodness. Calvin thought he might die of happiness. Nobody was in sight, though surely the camp's attendees would return in short order. He'd have to be quick.

He instantly wished he'd never bothered.

The toe of one boot had only just crossed the edge of the clearing when the fire completely vanished, taking the meat and its divine scent with it. In its place were three grown men, all wearing mages' robes and pointing wands at him. Hoods concealed their faces from their brows to their noses, leaving only their leering smiles exposed to the light.

"No!" Calvin gasped.

"Gotta love the illusory charms, eh Rupert?" said one mage, his homestead accent thick.

"You can definitely catch new dogs with old tricks, Niles," said another.

Calvin seized, unable to believe he'd fallen for this. Who in their right head would leave such a glorious cut of meat on a spit where the fire could ruin it? He'd been warned back at Mount Vernon not to fall for obvious illusory charms—think things through, find the fault, don't jump into an open trap. Had he thought about it for three more seconds, he might have known!

"*Onstyrian gestillan,*" said the third mage, casting a spell. Against his will, Calvin's body went completely rigid, ignoring his every attempt to move. He stood as steady and still as a statue from the neck down.

"No! Stop, I didn't do anything!" Calvin said.

Rupert and Niles casually lowered their wands and threw back their hoods, but their companion held still, wand trained on Calvin.

"Hold, mates. Sump'n about that voice." With a flourish, the third mage threw his hood back. His face had been scarred on one side by fire and intense pressure. The skin had healed somewhat, but the disfiguration couldn't be fully remedied. Calvin's eyes locked on that face, on the side unmarred by whatever had burned him. Dread gripped his soul.

It was Hammond Birtwistle.

"Tell me again how you din't do nothin'," Birtwistle seethed. He touched a finger to his cheek. "This a whole lot of nothin' to you?"

"You were dead," Calvin whispered. "The grenade . . ."

"Gave me this face!" Birty snarled. "*You* gave me this face!

Tintreg!"

Calvin screamed. A full-body torment punched him right in the head and got worse from there. Fire, ice, pins, needles, cuts, and blows all at once. There was a time when it would have permanently crippled him, but his newfound familiarity with extreme pain only made it last longer. Worse yet, the paralysis spell kept him upright, unable to do anything but suffer it until Birtwistle diverted his wand. The pain lingered, and Calvin panted until it ebbed.

"Right then, so Hammond has a history with this one," Niles observed.

"I didn't see no torture curse. You see a torture curse, Niles?"

"Not I, Rupert."

"We gonna have fun with this one then, boss?"

Birtwistle didn't reply. His steely gaze remained on Calvin, his demeanor taut, like he was debating whether to use the torture curse again. Calvin could only hang his head, breathing hard, wishing that one of them would just kill him and be done with it. Maybe he'd come far enough, anyhow. Some relief was more than welcome.

Death. He could live with that.

And yet, it was not to be.

"Put him with the others!" Birtwistle ordered. "I think our haul's good enough for one day, mates."

"Sounder judgment I've never heard, Hammer," said Rupert.

Birtwistle rolled his eyes at the nickname and trudged off. The two junior mages worked more magic on Calvin, turning out his pockets with invisible spells to confirm he wasn't armed. Once assured, Niles took Calvin's hand and touched his wand to Calvin's right wrist.

"*Unnytt.*"

An intricate geometric glyph appeared on Calvin's skin, inky and black as night. His hand went dead, unresponsive, limp as a day-old fish. Rupert duplicated the spell on Calvin's other hand. With additional charms, they levitated him to a nearby wagon he hadn't previously noticed, a simple four-wheeled contraption with an iron frame, a wooden body, and a canvas top. It had a conductor's bench up front but no reins, no horses. Birtwistle sat in the middle, looking angry and bored at the same time.

The mages threw Calvin into the open rear of the wagon. He landed unceremoniously atop three other prisoners, who by his reckoning had been asleep.

"*Heoloohelm weall!*" Rupert declared. This charm was directed at the back of the wagon, which had no rear door.

"Don't you just love that look in their eyes, Rupert? Like you can *see* them thinking how easy it'll be to give us the slip," Niles said.

"Almost makes me want to stay and watch, Niles. Hey, boy! Just so's you don't make trouble back there, we done took away them hands a'yours. We also done charmed the wagon so's you can't make off without our wanting you to. This is home for a few days. Get used to it." Rupert cackled triumphantly, and the two of them disappeared from sight.

"You mind getting your knee outta my ribs?" asked a voice near his ear. The speaker had a Merykan accent.

"Sorry," Calvin said. The word felt strange on his lips.

As the prisoners struggled to untangle themselves, Calvin rolled off and studied his markings. The mages hadn't lied; he couldn't move anything past his wrists. His hands and fingers hung limply, unresponsive, as though asleep.

"Just my luck," he muttered to himself. He was furious, but he wasn't surprised. Not yet.

"Well, ain't it a day for reunions," said that same voice. "Hey Dan, you recognize this kid? Baltimore, right?"

Frowning, Calvin squinted in the dim light of the wagon, and got his first look at the others, recognizing their faces one by one. Under no circumstances could he have been less pleased to see them.

They sat against the sides of the wagon, their ankles bound in irons, their wrists marked with the same paralysis enchantments. Calvin matched their faces to their names in his memory: Griff Cade, Daniel Aberforth, and John Penn. The very trio that had tricked him into joining the technomancers.

Calvin searched for the right thing to say, for the most accurate conveyance of the rage that so easily blossomed within him. Nothing sufficed. As he trembled with fury, Penn just shook his head and sighed, leaning back.

"Save it, kid. We're all in the same briar patch today."

"No thanks to you!" Calvin tried to kick Penn, but the wagon was too cramped. He only succeeded in falling over, causing his cheeks to flush with embarrassment.

"*Onbringan,* let's move!" said Birtwistle from outside. A spell took effect and the wagon rolled of its own accord, carrying them to an unknown destination.

EDITH MCCRACKEN

CHAPTER 13

Though she was accustomed to believing in things that other people didn't, Amelia wondered what she'd eaten that had made her dream of a thunderbird. Mom had told her stories about crossing paths with the giant fowl in her early days as a mimic pilot. They'd been more plentiful back then. Kings of the sky, she'd said. Vibrant in color—the males red, the females blue—and endowed with ferocious powers from nature, they were a sight to behold. Nowadays their numbers had dwindled to the point where some people doubted they'd ever existed in the first place.

For a long moment after she awoke, Amelia could almost *see* the bird flying along the course of a river at dusk, a massive male with a small human figure astride its back. His clothes were rags,

157

and the wind pulled at his shaggy blond hair. There was a familiarity to his posture, a profile she'd seen half a dozen times while secretly watching the last class of recruits . . .

Calvin! She'd definitely been dreaming, then. She sighed and resigned herself to a prolonged spell of attempted sleep, and had just begun to doze again when the muted exhaust of a dragonling mimic reached her ears.

Stirring, Amelia slid out of bed and went to the window. Icy black night covered the view and clouds concealed most of the light from the moon, so the dim amber glow of a lantern in the stables stood out to her. A messenger?

The light in the stables went out, and she could barely see three silhouettes crossing the lawn to the house: Peter, Brian, and a technomancer pilot. They'd be headed for Dad's study where they'd receive news from the other outposts.

Maybe there would be something about Calvin. Maybe.

Amelia hitched up her nightgown and dashed over to the closet on the balls of her feet, stepping only on the floorboards she knew wouldn't make a sound. She tied up the excess length of her gown with a sash—it was practically impossible to crawl in a dress—and retrieved a key from her jewelry box. In the back of the closet there was a short, square door which she unlocked and pulled aside. A musty breeze issued forth out of the dark space beyond. She plunged into it.

According to the stories, George Washington had commissioned Mount Vernon's architect to build a network of secret corridors in the house for purposes of smuggling and espionage.

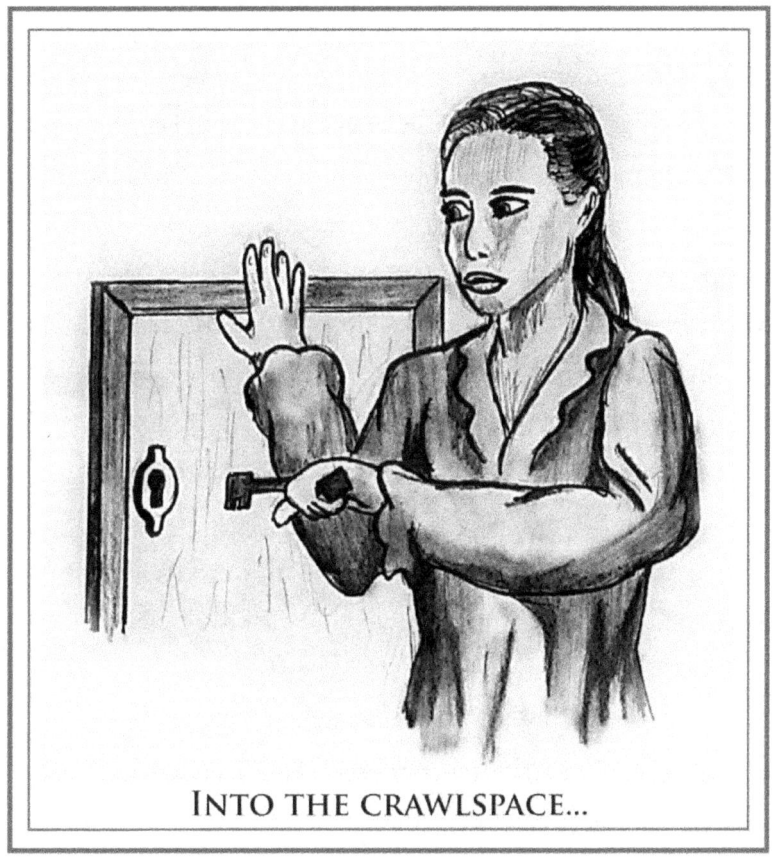

INTO THE CRAWLSPACE...

The only places the network didn't lead were the brig and the front foyer, neither of which were her destination. Crawling the whole way, she turned left at a junction, shimmied around a tight corner and gently crept to an open grate that serviced Dad's quarters. Slowing her breathing, Amelia froze and listened.

The door opened. Peter and Brian escorted the messenger into the old bedroom—history noted that it had belonged to Nelly

Custis, the step granddaughter of George Washington. Now it served as Dad's office, with two windows on one side and a well-tended fireplace in the corner. The walls were bare, and the only piece of furniture was a large oak desk in the middle of the room, covered with papers and books and maps of the continent.

"Technomancer Contessa Delinois reporting, Commodore," the pilot said, pulling Dad's attention away from his work. Amelia repositioned herself to get a better look at Contessa; she was a lovely dark-skinned woman, probably from the island nation of Haiti, given her name and accent.

"Intel updates?" Dad asked.

"*Oui*, Commodore."

"What's the short version?"

"It's bad. Lord Crutchley has taken the threat seriously—there's some political posturing behind it, trying to earn favor from the King and all that, so—"

Dad cut her off. "What are their numbers?"

Contessa fished through her pockets. Amelia tried to get a look at the papers she produced, but couldn't do so without exposing too much of her face behind the grate. Of what she could see, the writing was intentionally garbled. Chicken scratch to the untrained eye.

"Two thousand additional combat mages of standard rank," she began.

"That's not too bad," Brian said. Dad silenced him.

"Sixteen hundred Redcloak Elites," Contessa continued.

"*That's* bad," said Peter.

"Four hundred staff-men from the Scottish Highlands, and an equal count of mercenaries out of Hesse, Germany." Contessa passed her notes to Dad. "And the spies say Crutchley is floating the idea of commissioning the Draconic Trifecta when they learn the location of the *Saint George*."

"You mean *if* they find it, TechMan," Dad corrected her. "Don't underestimate Major Tyler. She's shrewd and resolute; she'll find a way to keep it hidden until we call for her. Even I don't know where it is right now."

Contessa shifted nervously. "*Bien sûr*, Commodore."

Amelia searched her memory. She'd heard of something called the *Saint George*, but whatever it was, Dad had guarded the secret well. What could it do, that it scared the Brits bad enough to bring in the descendants of the three dragons that had executed Washington himself?

For the next half an hour, Contessa brought Dad up to speed on the goings-on elsewhere across the land. Apparently something horrible had happened at a TechMan camp in the Ohio country— the mages had found it and had attacked with a degree of savagery that hadn't been seen in some time. The TechMan survivors had fled to Pittsburgh where they'd teamed up with Major Glenshaw's army. Whatever this *Saint George* was, it had been in Youngstown, and thus was the cause of great concern.

Better news came out of the south, where Major Yahola's army had successfully armed a band of Spanish technomancers. It didn't sound like they used mimics, but they did have machinery they'd dubbed "war wagons." Amelia tried to imagine what those were. And up north in Trenton, Major Aberforth had salvaged more mimics than expected, bolstering the number of battle-ready machines for some large-scale event. She'd heard them talking about it before, but it sounded like the schedule had changed? Why?

"All accounted for, it's not as hopeless as I feared," Dad said, rolling a pen back and forth in his fingers, eyes scanning the documents on his desk. "You did well by bringing this tonight. Boys, fetch refreshments for the lady. Contessa, you're welcome to stay and get a full sleep."

The pilot palmed her tired eyes. "Oh, but that'd be a treat, Commodore. *Merci.*"

Peter and Brian led her out. Amelia stayed until Dad had placed all of the documents in a folder, which he then placed in a strong box. He'd take that box out to his mimic sometime the next morning. When it wasn't in his office, it was in the mimic, and she hadn't yet discovered its hiding place there.

When Dad left his desk, Amelia retreated in the crawlspace, taking care to remain as quiet as possible. She exited the network through a different door and escaped into the hallway, intercepting Dad on his way to his room.

"I know you were there," he said as soon as he saw her.

Her shoulders slumped in defeat. "What gave it away?"

A proud smile pulled at one side of his mouth. "You are your mother's daughter. That, and you've soiled your gown."

Amelia looked down at her night gown and slapped her forehead; the sash was still in place, and the fabric was dark with dust where it had dragged. She hadn't cleaned the crawlspace in recent memory.

"Are you mad?"

"Not remotely, love. I don't think it will hurt for you to hear *some* of the things your brothers know," Dad said, pulling her into a gentle hug.

"But why not all of it?" Amelia squeezed him tight and felt him let out a little sigh of frustration. He'd answered her on this before, yet she still hoped that he'd change his mind.

"Because there are certain things that a nation should hold on to, and protecting the fairer sex is one of them. Your brothers are soldiers, Amelia. It is a man's duty to go out and fight so that the women in his life don't have to. I don't want that future for you."

"What if I want it?"

"You can do better than that. No, don't look at me that way Amy, I'm serious. You have a great mind and a passionate spirit . . ."

"And I can put those things to use changing diapers and baking pies?"

Dad sighed again. "Motherhood is a noble calling, and combat is no place for a lady. Leave the fighting to me and your brothers," he said.

"You let young girls join all the time. Two of them were in

Calvin's group."

Dad's right eye twitched at the mention of his name. Amelia pulled back and furrowed her brow.

"What? What is it?"

"It's nothing, my dear."

"No, I saw that. What is it about Calvin? You've gotten news, haven't you?"

Dad waved her off. "He's just another soldier. He's nobody. His name came across my desk on a desertion report last week—we dispatched him to the Ohio country, only to learn that he was brittle at the spine. Now he's—"

"Not with the army." Amelia looked away, deep in thought. If he'd deserted, would he come for her? And wouldn't he have to do so by some means other than a mimic?

The thunderbird . . .

Dad placed his hands on her shoulders and leaned over, his eyes level with hers.

"Amelia, I know young love is a tender thing. I know that what I am saying is not what you want to hear. But if you believe nothing else that I say, I beg of you to believe that I only want the best life for you. I will keep you out of combat, I will lead this revolution to its rightful conclusion, and I will help you choose a *worthy* suitor when the time comes.

"Until then, please, forget about that boy. He is gone."

Tears streamed down her cheeks. She didn't trust herself to speak. Dad averted his eyes—the right one twitched again—and planted a soft kiss on her forehead.

Amelia went back to her room and closed the door, unsure of what to do next.

She hated it when Dad lied.

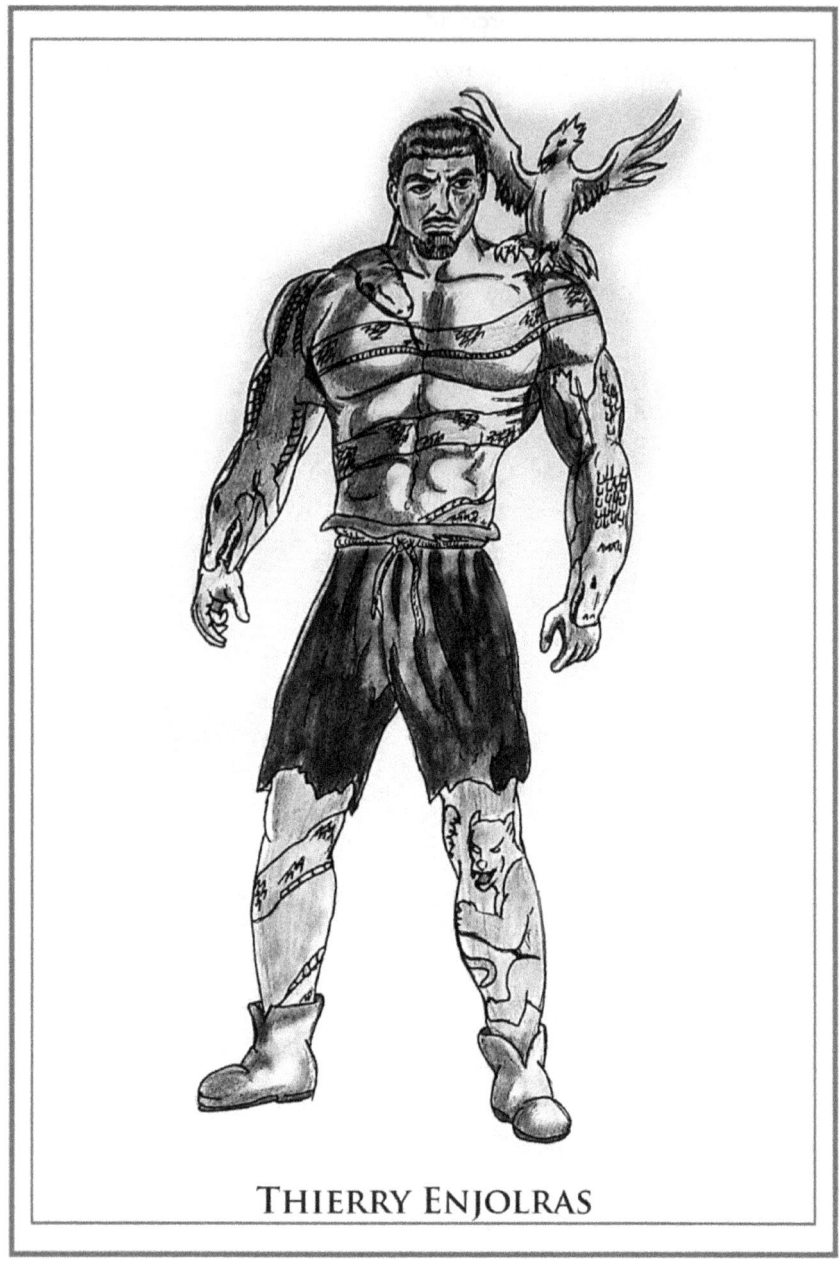

THIERRY ENJOLRAS

CHAPTER 14

The teleportal network had proved troublesome; Godfrey had almost drawn the attention of a mage officer back in Port Atlantis, so they had to move more slowly for a while. Three agonizingly long days later, they reached another swamp, and Kalfu took Godfrey to meet his contact.

When the man emerged from his moldy, moss-covered house, Godfrey suddenly felt much better about their chances of capturing Calvin Adler.

The alligator hunter stood nearly six and a half feet tall, and his body was thick with muscles. Calluses armored the palms of his hands, the result of years of tugging on thin cords with violent river monsters hooked at the other end. He had slick black hair, and a small army of exquisite tattoos covered his bronzed skin.

It was the tattoos that gave it away—the gator slayer was a pictomancer, skilled in the art of, well, *art* as a form of magic. Most likely those tattoos weren't permanent, but rather magical constructs that could stand up and walk off of his skin with a single command.

"Maitre Carrefour! Qu'est-ce que vous faites ici?" the pictomancer asked, speaking French with an outrageously thick accent. He could only be Cajun, an ex-patriot of the French-controlled Quebec region. This was . . . an alarming development. Quebec was where France sent all their undesirables, and Louisiana was where they went when Quebec didn't want them.

A criminal too harsh for a land of criminals? This man was not to be trifled with.

Kalfu responded to the Cajun man in kind, though Godfrey didn't understand French with any great degree of fluidity. Squeezing Fitz's badge, he probed it with his magic and found an equation for omnilinguism, which he cast over his own ears. Kalfu's words switched to English halfway through his introduction.

"—British kid, trying to make a name for himself. Oh, and he can understand us now."

Godfrey rolled his eyes. Did Kalfu know *everything* that happened around him?

"His name's Godfrey Norrington, of the Royal Mage Corps.

Godfrey, this is Thierry Enjolras," Kalfu went on.

Thierry crossed his arms over his huge chest and looked Godfrey up and down, assessing him with a harrumph. He spat on the ground. "Mage? He's just some kid."

Godfrey bristled at that, and tapped Fitz's badge again, chasing a hunch. Thankfully Fitz had been stationed near the border before, and had known some useful things about French prison culture.

"That ink on your knuckles; you got it at the Donnacona Institution. It's the signature marking of *Les Diables Blancs,* a Cajun prison gang."

Thierry cracked a smile. "So you've seen some things."

Sure, let him think that. "You've done time up north."

"Well I sure didn't come this far south for the scenery."

"I prefer the scenery in New Britain, personally. Looks a lot better than this hell hole. You can cross the border with help from the right man," Godfrey suggested.

"*Mais, non.*" Thierry shook his head. The dismissal was so clear, Fitz' badge didn't see a need to translate it. "There's no gator trade up in Meryka. That's what I do."

"I can get you gold."

"I don' work for money."

Godfrey pointed at a pile of dead gators on a nearby wagon. "What's this, then?"

"Trade 'em for favors. People like the meat or the skin." Thierry hooked his thumbs in the armholes of his vest. His entire wardrobe was made of gator leather.

Godfrey sighed. "Kalfu, I'm a mage. I don't deal with favors, you know that." Doing someone a favor was a highly volatile form of currency, and it wouldn't do for a mage to be beholden to someone for anything, least of all on such a shady deal as this. *Leave the favors to the fae;* that was one of the principle rules he'd learned at the Ipswich School.

"And what do you want in all of this?" Thierry asked Kalfu. "What's so great that you're running 'round down here with a Brit?"

"He's tracking a special quarry, my interest lies there. We need your help to subdue him—I want a sample of his blood, and Godfrey wants the bounty on his head."

Folding his arms again, Thierry tapped a finger against his bicep, thinking it over. Godfrey shifted his weight impatiently. Then Thierry spoke.

"Your badge, then. An object, not a favor." He stuck his chin out, using it to indicate Fitz's badge on Godfrey's robes.

"What?" The idea of a mage's badge in the hands of a delinquent was unpleasant.

"That's my price."

Godfrey considered it. The badge had been useful thus far, and while he was loathe to part with it, he wouldn't need it once he had Calvin Adler in custody. He knew the way back to Vauxhaul Outpost by heart.

"Fine," he said. "But only after we have captured my quarry.

This badge and nothing else will be your payment."

Thierry clucked his tongue. "*Très bien.*" They shook on it.

Leaning on his staff, Kalfu worked his magic on what little amount remained of Calvin's blood. He stood there for a minute, his white eyes glassy and unfocused, lips moving silently as he spoke to himself.

"By Merlin," Godfrey moaned. "How'd he move so far in a week? He must be on a machine again."

"He is moving slowly now, though. Has been for a while." Kalfu knitted his brow. "He is very badly injured, near death, even. Strange things are happening to his heart. I have never seen this before."

"Well yeah. You blind," Thierry grunted.

"You stick to your scribbles," Kalfu said. "Get me a map."

"Got better than a map." Thierry disappeared into his swamp house and returned a moment later with a heavy atlas, hand drawn on sheets of high-quality vellum. Kalfu muttered some magic words under his breath, and the reading of his spell translated into marks on the map. The three magicians huddled over the open atlas and considered the new information.

"There's a teleportal not far from here. It's been long enough, we should risk it." Godfrey tapped a space on the map, wishing he had his wand. Thierry leered at Fitz's badge again, smiling.

"Good. You take care a' that thing now, yeah?"

"You just worry about your part, convict. I'll do mine."

"Let us hurry." Kalfu said, shifting his staff to his other hand.

He sounded worried. "He's no good to us dead."

*

John Penn actually had the nerve to doze off in the wagon. Calvin could do no such thing; Hamilton's dial throbbed with every bump in the road, keeping him awake.

Thoughts of Amelia, of their fate, and of the hopelessness of his situation didn't help much either. Frustrated and with no other outlet, he shifted his weight to the right and kicked John hard in the ribs.

"Ow!" John snapped awake, trying to cradle his side with a limp hand.

"Whoops. Must've twitched in my sleep," Calvin said.

Griff and Daniel stirred and woke as well, struggling with their restraints. John told them to relax.

"You think kicking me is going to improve our situation, Adler?"

Calvin shrugged. "Feels good."

"You got no right to be upset, kid. You wanted to fight mages, and we made it happen."

"Great work, John. That's why I'm here with you three jackasses."

"You're *here* because *you* messed up. Yeah, I know all about Youngstown. The Majors keep us in the loop while we move. Don't take your sins out on us," John said.

"How can you sleep, knowing that you use people to fight a war that won't change anything?" Calvin demanded.

172

"Your delusion isn't my problem. We needed an army, so we made one. We didn't have time to wait for you to be okay with that."

"Guess not, King Charles," Calvin said.

John Penn actually chuckled. "Throw fits all you like, but our system worked, until you broke it. Now everything is wrecked. They're rounding up anyone they suspect of technomancy, and they're taking us to who-knows-where for magical interrogation. None of us is going to survive that, just so you know."

"It wasn't enough for you to be a deserter, Calvin?" Griff added.

"You know how many decades of hard labor you undid? How many sacrifices you wasted?" said Daniel.

"Deserter? You think I'm walking around out here 'cause I wanted to?" It took a few tries, but Calvin hooked a lame thumb through the V-collar of his stolen shirt and pushed it aside to show them the device. The recruiters' eyes widened in a mix of horror and recognition.

"That thing's gonna kill you," Daniel said, dumbfounded.

"Thanks, genius. Compliments of Captain Hamilton, on Major Tyler's orders." Calvin let his hand fall free, concealing his plight again. "This isn't desertion, it's a suicide run. Don't waste time thinking I feel bad for any of *you*."

"Likewise," John said. "They gave you what, nine, ten days? That's more than you deserve for exposing the *Saint George*. I cannot *believe* the level of stupidity . . . what could possibly have been worth that?"

A wry smile formed on Calvin's face. "There was something I needed to do. Didn't have time to wait until you were okay with it."

*

The teleportal deposited Godfrey onto a road that, while well-traveled, hadn't yet been paved. It cut through a wooded area and eventually connected to an intercolonial thoroughfare. Fitz's badge said that the surrounding wilderness had been favorable to traveling duffer spies in years past, which explained why Kalfu had detected Calvin moving steadily down this road for many hours now.

"Conceal yourselves," Kalfu ordered, taking shelter in a thicket some yards off the path. Thierry and Godfrey hid on the opposite side of the path behind a stand of weeds, so as to ambush Calvin from multiple angles. He noticed Thierry rummaging through his pack of art supplies; the pictomancer was about to cast something.

Minutes passed, and Godfrey kept his eyes glued to a bend in the road, expecting Calvin to come limping into view any moment now. When the procession finally arrived, it was not what he had expected.

"Enchanted carriage," he whispered to Thierry, who was mumbling to himself as he sorted through different pieces of magical charcoal sticks.

"Thought he was a duffer?" the pictomancer said, distracted.

"He is. I count three mages riding on the front, so maybe they took him prisoner? Oh, bollocks!"

"What?" Thierry looked up from his work.

"That's Birtwistle in the middle. Sod all, I thought he was dead!" Godfrey looked over at Kalfu, trying to get the sangromancer's attention. Kalfu just sat there, legs crossed and arms folded, his staff resting on his knees. He might have been asleep. Godfrey clenched his hands into fists.

"Calvin was supposed to be alone! Bugger, this complicates things," he said.

"Nope. It doesn't." Thierry unrolled a sheet of gator leather on the dirt and began sketching on it with an inexhaustible quill. His eyes were closed, and he used his pictomancy to illustrate the scene down the road where Birtwistle and his party were about to be. Godfrey watched Thierry work, intrigued.

The drawing had amazing detail, almost like a photograph cast in black and white upon the leather. It was a perfect match at first, but then Thierry drew the back of the wagon without a cover, so as to detail the occupants inside. Three were grown men, and the fourth was Adler.

"Seven in all," Thierry said. "Three mages. Four duffers. That wagon's charmed with a one-way screen all around. Stuff goes in but don't come out 'less they say so."

"Standard, for a prison transport. You'd know your way around one," Godfrey said.

"Then let this impress you, *peeshwank*." Thierry ran his quill in a flawless circle around the sketch of the road. Then he hastily illustrated three little figures outside the circle—near-perfect approximations of Godfrey, Kalfu and Thierry himself.

PICTOMANCY

"What are the rules for this?" asked Godfrey. Pictomancy was a very precise discipline, like drawing a story to life and watching it play out.

"Long as this drawing is intact, we're the only ones who can move in or out of the circle. They won't notice right away that they keep covering the same stretch of ground," Thierry said.

"Good. First we dispatch the mages, then the other duffers. I'll break the charms on the wagon, we get away with Adler, we square up, and we part ways. Let's go."

Across the way, Kalfu stood as if he'd been right there with them, conspiring at the same time. The trio spread out around the perimeter of the circle, equidistant from one another. Kalfu folded his arms and bowed his head, never taking his milky eyes off the approaching carriage, while Thierry shrugged out of his leather vest and closed his eyes, entering a trance. Godfrey coveted the way that the two mancers could so easily practice their magic without a focusing instrument; not for the first time, he missed his wand.

Thierry muttered a command in Cajun French. Two huge alligator tattoos swirled on his torso, writhing and twisting to life. Slowly they pushed against Thierry's skin as if they were beneath it, thrashing harder and harder until they stood up and perched on his flesh like lizards. When they sprang off of him and belly-flopped onto the ground, they grew to full size, though they had a mildly translucent quality about them. Where the tattoos had been, Thierry now had unblemished flesh.

The massive gators sauntered down the road, seconds away from intercepting Hammond's new crew. Thierry concentrated on summoning more monsters to go with them; a firebird sprouted from his back, eight wasps from his knuckles, and a huge serpent uncoiled from around one leg. The many constructs shoved their way into the brush and hovered at the edge of Thierry's circle spell, waiting for a command.

Once, twice, three times the carriage passed through the circle charm, covering the same stretch of ground repeatedly. Godfrey had never been on the receiving end of such a charm and didn't know how it looked from the inside; there must have been something to conceal the sudden shift as one walked through a portal that projected you thirty feet backward.

"*C'est bon,*" Thierry said. "*Attaque!*"

The picto-beasts launched their attack.

In shambled the gators. One of them threw itself bodily at the carriage and latched its massive jaws on the front wheel, stopping it fast, while the other gator reared up and lunged at the mages up top. To their credit, the mages rapidly constructed their own shield charms and repelled the beast before it could do them in.

One mage fell off the carriage, hit the ground, and tried to run for the woods, but Thierry's circle spell kept him contained. The picto-python slithered after him and soon had him in its coils.

"Don't kill him," Godfrey urged.

"He is only a mage," Thierry spat, eyes still shut.

Godfrey stayed crouched, waiting for the right moment to join the fight. Thierry's wasps had engaged the other new wizard, who tried to swat them away, but they were too many and they stung him over and over. Birtwistle uttered a repellent spell with his wand to drive them away, only to be struck in the back by a pictomantic firebird. The collision knocked his wand loose, and the slight contact set fire to his robes. As Birty panicked and swatted at the flames, Godfrey stole forth into the circle and seized the fallen wand.

"You and yours hold tight, and this don't have to get worse than it is!" he shouted.

Birty momentarily forgot his smoking robes, jerking his head around at the sound of Godfrey's voice. His eyes lit up with recognition and hatred. "You! You deserted!"

"It's a touch more complicated than that, mate. Give me your prisoners and it'll all make sense in a couple of days." Godfrey raised the wand to show he was serious.

"I've got a better idea!" Birty reached into his companion's robes and swiped his wand, leveling it at Godfrey with a curse on his half-burned lips.

"What? Wait, don't!" Godfrey shrieked.

"Heofonfyr!"

A white-hot geyser of flame issued forth from the wand. Just as quickly as it had formed, Thierry's picto-phoenix flew between Godfrey and the fire curse, absorbing the full brunt of it into the center of its body. The phoenix hovered in the air, its innards churning, and then it belched the fire back at Birtwistle three times stronger.

Birty screamed as the inferno reduced him to ash in seconds.

"No! Why'd you do that!" Godfrey roared at Thierry. The pictomancer edged closer to the circle, directing his creations with subtle movements of his hands. The snake and the gators held the other two mages at bay, smothering them so that they couldn't speak.

"He was going to burn you," Thierry said.

"I can deflect a *heofonfyr* curse! Bloody hell, man!"

Thierry shrugged his big shoulders. "Didn't want him to melt that badge."

Birtwistle . . . he was dead! Just like that!

"Come now, *mon fils*," Kalfu said, walking past Thierry to the rear of the wagon, the butt of his staff thudding against the ground.

"Let's finish our work."

Struck dumb by Thierry's actions, Godfrey just shook his head and went after Kalfu. He couldn't wait to rid himself of these two.

"What's happening out there?" Calvin asked. Screams and shouts jostled the four prisoners out of the drudgery of their voyage. For the hundredth time Calvin tried to shake the feeling back into his hands.

"They're under attack. Damn, this could be bad." Penn shifted onto his knees, trying to peer through the smallest hole in the wagon canvas.

"Is it technomancers?" Daniel asked.

"I don't hear any motors. Or gunshots," Griff said.

"If anyone's been sitting on a special secret cure for these wrist charms, now's the time!" John Penn said.

Footsteps crunched outside, coming to the open rear of the wagon. A man with a dark face appeared there, framed in a mess of gray-and-white dreadlocks, his eyes as white as snow. He wore messy robes of shredded cloth and woven fish nets. He smiled wide, the smile of a predator, and his teeth and gums were a bright white. The stench of blood filled the air.

"Oh, hell! Sangromancer!" Griff shouted.

Calvin didn't know what to do, and even if he had, he doubted he could have done it in his current state. The sangromancer raised a gnarled hand and pointed a finger at the dial in Calvin's chest. In deep, ominous tones he began chanting in a language Calvin didn't know.

Invisible needles pricked his chest, hot and sharp, wringing sweat from his skin. A burning pain shot into his very core, along with a sick feeling that made Calvin want to vomit. Whatever the sangromancer was doing, it was *bad*. He found himself swatting at the dial with his limp fingers, a purely instinctive defense that had no hope of working.

"Stop!" he screamed, thrashing about, his muscles seizing.

"Hold on to yourself, Calvin! He'll try to take your soul, just hold on!" John said as he tried to shove the back door open.

A deluge of foreign images flooded Calvin's mind, like water bursting through a dam, carrying memories that were not his own—memories that belonged to the sangromancer.

Kalfu LeVeau.

Yes, that was his name. A master manipulator of blood who'd prolonged his unnatural life by consuming the life force from valuable specimens—people of relentless passion, people whose hearts beat wildly with love and knew many shades of pain and dread. Kalfu was old, very old, and had done this many times before to keep going.

Calvin was next. As he succumbed to a mental fog, he slumped to the floor, the world spinning about in a dizzying spiral. His mind reeled the way it had upon first contact with Karahkwa the thunderbird.

Exactly like that.

Wait . . .

That familiar sensation bubbled up in Calvin's consciousness, identified neither by image nor word, but by impression. At first the sangromancer's curses smothered it, but the impression grew stronger, more fervent, powerful enough to break the bravest heart. Was that . . . love?

"Non! C'est impossible!" the sangromancer roared. Then the connection between them shattered, seemingly for no reason at all, and Calvin's senses slammed back into him like a mimic at full speed. Gasping and blinking through a sudden sweat and fever, he recognized the deep, earth-shattering sound of a thunderclap at close range.

The roof of the wagon tore away to reveal the still waning light of dusk. A tangible burst of sound had shredded the canvas, leaving the wagon's four occupants staring upward in stunned alarm. Outside there came a panicked cry.

"Kill them! Kill them now!"

Of all the rotten luck, Godfrey had to run into a brace of thunderbirds.

Two of them dropped out of the sky—no warning, no provocation—and unleashed their shrill cry with pinpoint precision on Thierry's magic circle. The first thunderclap tore off the wagon's roof and put Kalfu flat on his butt; the second blast sidelined Thierry's beasties. Even with a wand, Godfrey had little means of defending himself; shield spells couldn't repel sound.

"Ne bougez pas!" Thierry roared. "Stay in the circle! I can fortify

it." He fumbled with a small pencil and a sheet of parchment from his back pocket. Before he could draw anything, the larger of the two birds—a red male—fired off another thunderclap at the drawing Thierry had left beside the road.

The gatorskin canvas burst into a thousand pieces, and the circle spell collapsed like broken glass.

KILL THEM NOW!

"Bollocks!" Godfrey ran for cover beside the wagon.

Thierry abandoned the parchment. He ordered his beasties to finish off Birty's companions, then steered them toward the incoming predator birds. With a final utterance in French, the magical constructs morphed and twisted together to form an unnatural monstrosity with scales, wings, claws, and poison.

It almost looked like a match for the thunderbirds.

"Kill them! Kill them now!" Godfrey said.

Behind the wagon, Kalfu pulled himself to his feet with his staff, shaking his head. Blood trickled from his ears and eyes. Godfrey crawled over to him.

"Are you hurt?" he asked.

"Look out!" Kalfu tackled Godfrey to the ground just as a thunderbird passed overhead. This one, a blue female, raked her hellish talons through the spot where Godfrey's head had been. Somewhere on the other side of the wagon, Thierry bellowed orders to his new monster, willing it to attack the red male.

"We have to go!" Godfrey said.

"Not yet!" Kalfu looked back at the wagon, its protective charms nullified by the damage. The technomancers piled out, flexing their fingers as if feeling them for the first time. Godfrey's heart sank—Birty and his companions would have put paralysis charms on them, and now that they were dead the magic was null. As feeling returned to the duffers' hands, they scrambled to freedom. One of them was fiddling with the contraband locker on the opposite side.

"Don't let them get their weapons!" Kalfu said. Flecks of blood and spittle flew from his lips—the thunderbird had not gone easy on him.

Godfrey pointed his new wand at the prisoner by the locker.

184

He had only formed the first syllable of a curse when the female thunderbird circled back and hit him with a targeted shriek, a tightly focused stream of air and sound that hit like a strong man's punch. The force lifted him off his feet and hurled him into a tree several yards back.

The world spun. He grimaced against the pain as the clearing came back into focus: Kalfu still leaned on his staff, uttering a healing spell, while the prisoners retrieved several duffer weapons from the contraband locker. The hated Calvin Adler appeared, bearing a frosted iron knife, looking intently at Kalfu with rage in his eyes. Off to Godfrey's left, Thierry held his ground, feet planted wide as he spun his arms in exaggerated motions, guiding his picto-monster in some semblance of a cockfight with the male thunderbird.

Try as he might, Godfrey couldn't form words. He pointed his wand at Calvin and tried some generic offensive spells, waving the tip this way and that, yet nothing came of it. He was too weak, too breathless to inflict any real damage.

One of the technomancers appeared with a recovered firearm and fired it four times at Kalfu—thrice in the heart, and once in the head. The force laid Kalfu out on the dirt, where he instantly became still. With the sangromancer down, the blue female rejoined her mate, and they struck at Thierry with a double-blast of thunder so powerful that it left a small crater in the ground. Even over the noise, Godfrey could hear Thierry's bones shatter and grind to dust. All of his pictomantic constructs faded, dispersing like fog before a rising sun.

And then there was only Godfrey. Panting, mind racing, he tried to figure out what to do next . . . where to go . . . where to hide . . .

"Wait a minute! You again?" Calvin pointed his iron blade at Godfrey. Any of his lingering hesitation over Kalfu's presence faded away, replaced by a look of sheer hatred. "You cut off my friend's hand!"

Right! Good idea. Godfrey tightened his quaking fingers around the wand and tried to summon up the energy for a *ceorfan* curse, but he was still too hurt from the thunderclap. Calvin Adler charged at him and batted the wand aside, then plunged his dagger directly into Godfrey's sternum. Godfrey howled as a pain like fire burned through his heart, spreading outward from the knife that jutted out of his chest. The poisonous metal extinguished the dregs of his magic, making his skin prickle and pull tight. An abrupt sensation of cold settled all the way to his core.

Calvin's fingers were still wrapped around the handle. He leaned in close and snarled, "This time do the smart thing and *die.*"

There was little Godfrey could make in the way of a counteroffer.

EHNITA

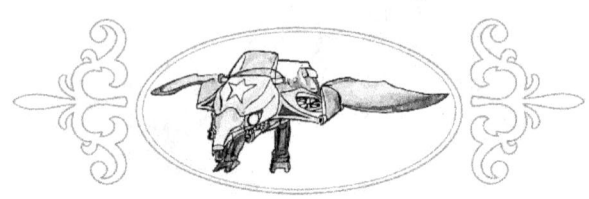

CHAPTER 15

Calvin willed himself to release the knife one finger at a time. The mage—*Godfrey Norrington, your personal headhunter*—slumped to the ground and gave up the ghost. As much as Calvin wanted to keep his knife, he couldn't bring himself to pull it out, as if doing so would revive him and they'd start this all over again. He bit his lip and turned his back on his most recent kill.

With the fighting over, the thunderbirds landed beside Calvin with a grace that he would not have attributed to creatures of their size. Karahkwa perched at a distance, standing upright in the presence of his mate. Ehnita, who was smaller with feathers of a bluish complexion, cautiously approached Calvin, head bobbing. Calvin held still as she lowered one eye to his face.

"Hello," Calvin said, fingers still shaking.

Ehnita's consciousness penetrated his mind, filling Calvin with duplicates of her own emotions—gratitude, admiration, even affection. They were appendages of a love truer than Calvin would have been able to describe with words.

"Love," Calvin breathed, as he drank in her thoughts.

Karahkwa joined in, his memories adding clarity to the big picture: after he'd dropped Calvin, he'd continued west until he reached Ehnita and told her that her stolen blood was destroyed. Yet Ehnita, seeing in Karahkwa's mind the whole story, insisted upon helping Calvin, who'd been instrumental in their reunion. Karahkwa had gleefully agreed. He'd do anything at her side.

Since Calvin had touched minds with him before, Karahkwa was able to find Calvin again, though it had taken some time. There was a hint of apology from the giant bird when he expressed this sentiment.

Calvin barked out a laugh. He wasn't sure what the sangromancer had wanted with him, only that he'd felt his life slipping away like wool pulled between his fingers. Their timing could not have been better.

Ehnita asked Calvin about his mate. He cocked an eyebrow, unsure what she meant, until she showed him the dream of Amelia that she'd seen in Karahkwa's memory. Just the sight of her in his mind made Calvin's knees go weak. He was about to answer Ehnita's question, but John Penn interrupted their reverie, clearing his throat more loudly than was necessary.

"We've got our gear." He spun the cylinder in his revolver and dropped it into his holster. Behind him, Griff and Daniel strapped their weapons on.

"That's nice," Calvin replied. He didn't move.

John tossed him a hat. "Here, this'll keep the sun off your head."

Calvin caught the hat but set it down without a word. John sighed.

"Do I have to paint a picture? We need to get to the . . ."

"Oh, I'm done with you, Penn. Thought you might have gathered that," Calvin said.

John growled and seized Calvin's arm. "You're still a TechMan, and you've got a desertion to answer for! Be that as it is, you'll—"

He was cut off when Ehnita sprang into the air and dropped her considerable weight onto John's chest, pinning him to the ground. Griff and Daniel grabbed their pistols, but hesitated to draw when Karahkwa reared up to his full height, his chest swelling with compressed wind.

"Y'all get the message?" Calvin asked. "Hands off the guns."

Griff and Daniel obeyed. Karahkwa exhaled slowly and tucked his wings back to his sides. His eyes never left the technomancers. At Ehnita's beckoning, Calvin came closer and stood over John, who was much more agreeable with a three-hundred-pound bird on his ribs.

"I'd like to kick you in the head right now," Calvin said.

John was unable to form a response.

"These birds are decent creatures, though. And it seems they

I'M DONE WITH YOU.

reward decency with decency. I'd rather ally with them than ever work for you and yours again, so accept my generosity and get out of here while you can. Any questions, Mr. Penn?"

John shook his head. Ehnita backed off and he scrambled away, fighting for breath as he rejoined his comrades.

"Where will you go?" Griff asked.

"Wherever I damn well please. You fight your war, I'll fight mine. That's the last I mean to say to you about it." Calvin folded his arms.

John considered the thunderbirds flanking Calvin; he seemed like he wanted to say something else, but he only scowled and walked off. Griff and Daniel followed him into the woods, disappearing like shadows in the night.

An air of contentment filled the space around Calvin; the sensation was so strong that he laughed aloud, causing the device to make his chest hurt again. Ehnita leaned closer so Calvin could rest against her shoulder.

"I need help," Calvin said, all bravado gone. "I need to go to Virginia. Do you know where that is?" He tried to think of Mount Vernon, tried to remember the smells and the stars, anything that would help them fix the location in their minds.

They responded with severe hesitance. Many of their kind had died that close to the ocean. They would be seen, shot, cursed out of the sky . . .

Calvin frowned. "Why the ocean?"

It wasn't the ocean; it was the shore. There was something in that general area, maybe fifty miles across—near the House of Commons?—and the thunderbirds were of the opinion that the people on the ground in that area didn't want it seen from the sky.

He filed that knowledge away, curious at its meaning. "I'm not headed to that place. There's a river, it's called the Potomac. Can you take me there by night?"

It seemed that was safer, but they still didn't know the exact location of Mount Vernon. Karahkwa shared a memory of a place west of Alexandria, where the sky smelled like Calvin and the technomancers. Calvin reviewed the memory and agreed that it had to be an outpost. By his best estimate, it was eighty miles west of Mount Vernon.

And they would probably have mimics.

"Let's go!"

They flew all night. An hour before dawn, Karahkwa and Ehnita dived down into the center of an expanse of farmland, one mile north of the outpost. It was as far as they were willing to go, and Calvin fell over himself to thank them profusely for what they'd done. As a way of bidding farewell, both of them in turn touched their foreheads to Calvin's, a gesture that felt like a hug he might have gotten from his parents. Then they took to the skies, and he watched them until they disappeared. His training at Mount Vernon had prepared him for many things, but meeting those two birds was by far the most surreal encounter of his life.

With their help, he'd done the impossible. He was only hours away from Amelia; looking down at his chest, he read the half-smudged numbers on the dial and saw that he had a little less than three days to spare. He was going to make it.

After tightening his boot laces, Calvin worked his way to the edge of the farm, found a road, and followed it to a small town. On the outskirts was a cluster of buildings that shone in the moonlight, which had to be the technomancer base. He took a moment to button his shirt all the way up to the collar; thankfully during his escapades he had only bled on the tunic underneath it, so nobody would inquire after his odd chest wound. Maybe Hamilton's devices weren't all that well-known, but it was better not to draw attention.

Two guards sprang on him from the bushes, rifles trained, demanding to know his identity. Calvin threw up his hands, having expected this, and gave them a prepared story about being a news runner for Camp Liberty, that he had intelligence he could only share with their commanding officer. Given the state of his clothes and the general aura of hopelessness that had hung on him since Hamilton first dropped him off the back of a mimic, it wasn't hard to sell the story. They blindfolded him and flew him on one of their own mimics (presumably so he wouldn't count his steps) to the front entrance of their encampment.

Like Liberty, this base—called Camp Winchester—was underground, though not as big. When the blindfold came off, Calvin faced a man who was older than Tyler but perhaps younger than McCracken. Streaks of gray colored his hair and scars decorated his face, neck, and arms. His clothing was neat and clean, and a mechanical appendage replaced one of his legs. He was a copper-skinned man, one of the native Merykan tribal members. There was something terribly familiar about the man's face, and then it hit him: he was the deckhand aboard the Boston merchant vessel all those years ago, the one who'd thrown a tomahawk with pinpoint precision at a pallet full of cargo, condemning it to a salty doom in lieu of surrendering it to the Crown.

Whoa, Calvin thought.

"I'm Major Yahola. Explain yourself," he said.

"Like I told your men, I'm out of Camp Liberty. Major Tyler sent me here from Pittsburgh as a news runner—our radio network was compromised." So far that was all true.

Yahola pursed his lips, his eyes unmoving. "What's your name?"

Calvin had thought of this. "Edsel Winford." It was a long shot, but he dared not give his own name.

Yahola looked over his shoulder at a subordinate, who had a sheaf of documents in hand. He flipped a few over, traced a finger down a page, and nodded at the Major. This seemed to mollify him.

"Last we heard from Liberty, they had to abandon the Ohio country. What happened?"

"Their cover was compromised. An army of mages moved in but we repelled them. Major Tyler led the survivors to Camp Monroe, and they've probably gone east since then. I've been out many days now." Also true, which helped him sell the story. He needed a favor from them, and he needed them to be on his side by the time he asked for it. "We had to tip our hand with respect to the *Saint George*, sir."

Yahola swore. Some of his cohorts murmured as well.

"It was nearly operational, too," Yahola moaned.

"Oh, they got it up and running, Major. Gave the mages quite a fright—sent them packing, even. I mean, the noise alone, to say nothing of the firepower . . ." Calvin trailed off as he remembered the sights and sounds of that horrible night.

Yahola closed his eyes and pinched the bridge of his nose, supporting himself on his desk with his other hand. "Keep going," he whispered.

"Sir?"

"The *Saint George*. Was she magnificent?"

"Beyond all comparison, and rightly so," Calvin said, his honesty surprising even himself. "Like a storm on legs, a real force of nature. Major Tyler said that if we act now, we can still gather together and protect it until we launch the prime offensive."

Yahola barked orders to the men behind Calvin. "Get every dragonling pilot up. I want a fleet of news runners in Pittsburgh an hour ago. They'll need our coordination. You, you're coming with me," he said to Calvin.

"All due respect, sir, I can't. I have orders from Major Tyler to personally warn Commodore McCracken about the situation. I meant to get to him first but I ran into a bit of trouble with some mages in Morgantown, and they dogged me all the way to Cumberland. I lost my mimic. Been stealing horses ever since, and I still have eighty miles to go," Calvin said, making it up as he went.

"We can radio Mount Vernon," Yahola said.

"No!" He hoped the severity in his tone would help sell his story. "No more radio! It's too risky, Major, sir. I think . . . I'm pretty sure that's how they found Camp Liberty."

Major Yahola stroked his chin. "I suppose that's possible. And if they know *Saint George* is out there, they'll want to track her movements any way they can."

"Yeah, and they can't know you've been warned. That's what Major Tyler said." He wished he'd thought up a more detailed lie beforehand, but Yahola's instincts had played to his favor. A small voice in Calvin's heart thanked whatever supreme force had decided to wake up and guide him these last few hours. Maybe he wasn't *entirely* without luck.

"Very well. Mount Vernon is only a few hours away by mimic. I will see if we can spare a gryphon pilot to take you there," Yahola said.

"I'll save you the pilot if you can spare me a dragonling," Calvin said.

Yahola was good for it. He ordered one of his lieutenants, a man called McDiarmid, to pull the oldest dragonling out of the motor pool and fuel it up for Calvin.

"I appreciate your adherence to Major Tyler's orders. The army is built upon the kind of determination and fortitude you've displayed, TechMan Winford," Yahola said as Calvin accepted a pair of goggles from a passing technician.

The captain's words stung, given what Calvin had just fed him. He tried to remind himself that his deception was a necessary evil.

"Just doing my duty, sir."

Yahola slapped a hand on the dragonling's fuel tank. "Try not to lose this one. Camp Liberty was our biggest factory, and now we'll have to take care of what few machines we currently possess."

"Absolutely, sir. I will see you again at Pittsburgh," Calvin said.

"Until then, Edsel."

Calvin emerged through a hidden exit gate and surfaced in a wheat field. Reading the compass on the handlebars by its illuminated markings, he steered south by southeast on a course for Mount Vernon.

All of the pain and anguish had been worth it now that he had a throttle in his hands and the wind in his hair. Amelia was close.

GODFREY NORRINGTON

CHAPTER 16

Heavy feet scraped over hard-packed ground. At least, it *felt* hard. Was it paved? He couldn't tell. Shuffle, shuffle, shuffle. Every step sent white-hot pain up his bones, and even through the fog engulfing his mind, it occurred to him that he was in bad shape.

Thump. Thump. Thump.

The staccato pain morphed into a constant ache. Why didn't he stop? That wasn't so hard, was it? But his legs just kept moving, broken only by the occasional prick of static on his skin, and a jarring sensation as though he were skipping across great distances in a single bound. Then he would land again, and the pain augmented. When it reached a certain point he opened his eyes, yet still trundled onward, bound for a murky bayou in the distance.

His vision blurred in and out of focus. His chest hurt. Was he breathing? Maybe. He wanted to throw up, but his guts didn't work. By all means he shouldn't even be upright. He had walked a great distance, yes, but he'd also hopped through teleportals along the way.

Teleportals. Something familiar about that.

He blinked. Whether by magical or mundane means, the distance shrank, and he was in the bayou. A shack stood before him.

It's not in the shack.

Right, that would have been too obvious. Where had he put it?

Put what? I didn't put anything . . .

Not you. Me.

He walked behind the shack to a pile of firewood. In a stump on the ground there was an axe. Yes, that was the place. He grabbed the handle and tugged it sideways.

Rather than pull free from the stump, the axe lifted the whole stump off the ground as if on a hinge, revealing a hidden shaft. He bent at the waist, groaning, and grabbed the edges of the hole to lower himself in. At the bottom he found a secret cave that extended under the house, lined with shelves along both walls and a workbench at the end.

I need light.

Fumbling with a set of matches, he lit a candle in the corner and set it by a mirror, which was pointed at more mirrors around the room. Soon the light filled the small place well enough for him to see his own reflection in the mirrors. His lungs didn't allow him to gasp, but the intention was there.

Godfrey's skin had turned a horrid shade of grey, mottled with blue specks where his blood had congealed in his veins. He expected his heart to race, his skin to flush, but these reactions were dead inside him. It made sense, after all: his heart was not beating.

Frowning, he lowered his eyes to a gaping knife wound in his chest, rimmed with bright red sores. When had he gotten that?

Adler.

That name . . .

The wound stung something awful. Not just his body, but his magic was affected by it. Weakened. Debilitated. Perhaps beyond the point of saving.

Oh, but you have much to learn about blood magic, I think, said the other voice. It sounded terribly familiar.

Kalfu! But . . . you're dead, Godfrey thought.

So are you. Get to work.

Godfrey's aching feet shuffled forward again. With one hand, he pulled up a corner of the carpet and rolled it back to the center of the room, revealing a square hole in the ground that housed a wooden chest. He extracted the chest and carried it to the workbench where he opened it and removed its contents. What was he going to do with this?

One does not live as long as I have without contingencies, Kalfu explained. *Open that box you're holding.*

202

The box held four large bottles inside, each one full of a thick, viscous substance that was dark in color. Some kind of sangromantic compound? A potion to preserve a blood sample? Labels indicated their content, the samples having been drawn from skilled magicians long ago. Pictomancy, sangromancy, psychomancy, necromancy.

Godfrey tipped each bottle into a cauldron, careful to extract every drop of the blood potions using Kalfu's fine tools. Then he selected other ingredients from the shelves, added them to the cauldron, and lit a fire under it. As he worked, Kalfu told him to utter various words from languages either long-forgotten or long-forbidden.

Some hours later, the concoction was complete. He drained it into an unused skin and stopped it tight, then secured it in a burlap sack, which he strapped to his back. Within minutes he had concealed the shop once more, climbed out of the hole, and retraced his long, slow, agonizing steps to the nearest teleportal outlet.

The fog retook his mind, releasing him only when he had returned to the place where he had died over twenty-four hours earlier. The wreckage of a wagon marked where the thunderbirds had freed the technomancers, a feat Godfrey couldn't explain. How could they control the birds? A most unsettling notion.

Six people had died here: one by strangulation, another by immolation, a third at the hands of some feral beast, a fourth had been positively *shattered* by a thunderclap, a fifth was riddled with bullets, and sixth was Godfrey. He walked over to Kalfu's corpse and stared down at his ruined torso for a moment, then got to work.

Again his vision left him, and while he felt his hands working on Kalfu's body, and he sensed strange words leaving his lips, he couldn't be sure what he was doing or saying. Kalfu's ghost tugged on invisible puppet strings in Godfrey's body, and whatever he was making Godfrey do, the self-pronounced voodoo god didn't want Godfrey to remember the process.

What an odd notion. Godfrey was dead. Did he have any plans for later?

How much time had passed? He couldn't tell. When his work was finished his vision clarified, and he was standing over Kalfu's body. A veritable atlas of strange symbols surrounded the sangromancer, drawn in the dirt with a twig by Godfrey's own hand. More glyphs and symbols adorned Kalfu's body, painted with the mixture Godfrey had put together in the workshop. The symbols swam before his eyes, refusing to adhere to his memory. Was he still muttering incantations? It felt like it.

He reached a hand down to Kalfu's forehead and felt a presence leave his own body, returning home to its proper vessel.

Godfrey staggered backward stiffly, still not fully in control of himself. A whirlwind of dust and magic surrounded Kalfu LeVeau, howling with terrible might, and when it settled down, the voodoo master stood on his feet again, shimmering with a dark aura.

"Thank you, Master Norrington," Kalfu said, flashing his

bright white teeth in a sinister leer. "I'd have done it myself, you see, but a man can be *too* broken. You know a great many of my secrets now. I would destroy most men for so much, but you and I still have a task to complete."

Godfrey's feet suddenly held in place. Kalfu extended a hand and cast a spell to reverse the damage to his heart, and as the magic worked, Godfrey caught a glimpse into Kalfu's mind, his memories, his true history. What lay hidden in there would have stunned even a lifelong practitioner of magic—mainly because Kalfu was too old to still be alive.

The sangromancer had left Africa almost three centuries ago, having been captured by slavers and brought to Meryka along with his brother. They were put to work in cotton fields, side by side, enduring their hardship by relying on one another. One afternoon his brother had tried to escape, only to be beaten to within an inch of his life by a warden. Kalfu had seen it all, crying out in anguish every time the whip struck his brother's flesh.

In magical terms, this caused a disjunction in Kalfu LeVeau, separating him from the barrier that suppressed his inert sangromantic powers. Up to this point in his life, Kalfu had assumed he was a duffer; his ensuing burst of power surprised him just as much as it did the warden, whose blood temperature soared until it boiled him alive from within. It was Kalfu's first blood curse.

Yet he learned blood curses were not devices of their own power; they drew from a nearby source. And there was plenty of blood on his brother's back. Though Kalfu had kept the whip from its final lash, he had unknowingly finished the job himself.

In his agony, Kalfu fled. He dedicated the rest of his days to the study of his newfound power. Years raced past, and as he interacted with other practitioners, he grew in power until he was the strongest and the wisest among them. From there, he began to experiment, at first reversing his old age, then later reversing dire injuries. He learned that he could use blood magic to control the minds and bodies of others, before, during, and after death. Those who he didn't intend to control, he drastically shortened their lives, draining the life force from their veins and adding it to his own.

And if his prey had special blood—like Calvin Adler—all the better.

What's special about Calvin's blood? What does it do for you?

Kalfu's laugh reverberated through Godfrey's hollow soul.

"Trouble not your mind, Godfrey Norrington. It is enough for you to know that I require you to capture him for me. In my current condition, I'm afraid I'm unable to accompany you personally in this task." Kalfu's dark aura wavered. Was he still injured? Sensing the unspoken question, he said, "No, not injured; I am still dead. I shall keep my mortal vessel with me until I can fully return. Fear not for my well-being; I have beaten death before."

Paralyzed with awe, Godfrey silenced any further thoughts.

"As for you, well, I think we've seen how you measure up against Adler in combat. You sorely lack any advantage over him.

UNFINISHED BUSINESS.

In return for the service you've just rendered, I give you a new lease on life . . .

". . . and the means to fulfill your purpose."

Godfrey dreamed of worms slithering through his skin, using his blood vessels like tunnels in mud. His veins and arteries squirmed throughout his whole body as they healed, realigned, and carried blood to his damaged muscles. Hours passed and when he regained consciousness, he sat up took stock of himself and his surroundings.

Trees. Brush. A wrecked wagon, a few dead bodies, and the remains of what had been a spell circle, before someone had wiped all the glyphs away.

"What the deuce?" he whispered.

And where had he gotten all of these tattoos? Two alligators, a phoenix, a serpent, and eight wasps?

His head ached something awful, and for the life of him he could not remember the last time he'd been conscious. Two days ago, maybe? He remembered a fight with the duffers in the Ohio country. They had a dragon machine. They repelled the mages.

Godfrey had fled . . . where? He got the sense that he hadn't been alone, and yet he was helpless to recall who might have been with him. And to add to the mystery, unknown magic swam inside him, powerful sorcery that begged to be cut loose. Pictomancy? That explained the tattoos, to an extent. That particular discipline had never been his strength, though.

Fighting down a panic attack, Godfrey drew in a deep breath and let it out slowly. He repeated this a few times, stood up, and got his bearings.

There was something he had to do, an itch that needed a hard scratch. It involved that duffer boy from Baltimore.

Calvin Adler.

More came rushing back to him. Not all of it, but enough of it.

Capture Calvin, stop the duffers, and return to England.

Yes! That was what he'd been on about.

"Right, then." Godfrey said, his words disrupting the otherwise silent air of the wood. "Time to get after it."

MAJOR YAHOLA

CHAPTER 17

Calvin flew at full throttle to Mount Vernon. The terrain rushed past in a blur of gray-green, the forest opening up every so often at a farm or village. These he circumvented, as he couldn't afford to get a trio of mages tailing him now that he was short on firepower. The mimic's belly cannons were loaded, but since they didn't fire aft, they were useless in an escape.

Mount Vernon loomed ahead, a whitewashed beacon against a tranquil backdrop of wilderness. He thought his heart might explode. When he was a quarter-mile out, he spotted Peter and Brian with a new group of cadets, most likely training for a farm raid. If Calvin was careful, he could land during one of their firing drills, hiding the mimic's exhaust noise.

He swung wide and came down low to make a shallow descent between the mansion and one of the adjacent houses. The mimic's landing legs cut twin gutters into the soft turf, and before it came to a full stop Calvin leapt out of the saddle and ran for the mansion, injuries and exhaustion forgotten, his need for Amelia outweighing all else. He shoved the door open and ran inside, unsure of where to look first. Would she be in the pantry right now? Or perhaps the lavatory? He had just grabbed the handrail at the bottom of the stairs when a deep voice called his name, making him flinch.

"Adler!" McCracken growled. "What the hell?"

Despite himself, Calvin cracked a smile. "Surprised to see me?"

"Hardly. Get out of my home."

"Not until I get what I came for, you two-tongued snake."

Leaning on his cane with one hand, McCracken drew a pistol from under his coat, cocked the hammer and aimed at Calvin's head. He was maybe twenty feet away; he wouldn't miss.

"Yours would not be the first blood that had to be cleaned off of these walls. Outside. *Now,*" the Commodore said.

Calvin narrowed his eyes, planting his feet firm and balling his hands into fists. "You don't know what it cost me to get here in the past week, old man. Unless you're going to kill me, you'll have to do worse than shoot me."

Commodore McCracken kept his composure, though he sighed dramatically and shook his head. "The fact that you made it here at all is quite a testament to your durability, I'll admit. And of course, were I to shoot you, my daughter might hear it and wonder what happened. I guess we'll have to settle for . . ."

A heavy weight struck Calvin from behind. Two arms snaked under his shoulders and behind his head, rendering his own arms useless. When his unseen attacker pulled tight, the device sliced through the damaged skin on Calvin's chest.

"Not tonight, scum!" It was Brian.

"You coward!" Calvin writhed and twisted, but Brian was in full health, and far stronger at the moment. He laughed at Calvin's futile struggle. Commodore McCracken holstered his gun and came closer, a condescending smile on his face.

"Here's a secret, Adler: nobody put me in charge of this army because I'm stupid. Boys, take him to the brig."

"*Amelia!*" Calvin screamed.

Too late; Brian spun Calvin around and brought him face-to-face with Peter, who held a stout wooden stick. He drew it back and clubbed Calvin hard on the head.

The world faded.

*

McCracken didn't like doing things this way, but a lifetime at war had deadened his conscience to it. The revolution would only succeed if hard men could make hard choices. He was a Sin Eater—the one who did bad things so that nobody else had to.

If the Adler boy had just done what he was told, he'd have avoided all of this.

"I assumed they'd have executed him," Peter said as he and

Brian carried Calvin's unconscious body down the stairs. McCracken followed them, navigating down the steps with his cane.

"Major Tyler had too much going on and didn't want the morale damaged by revealing what he'd done. Adler might have inspired sympathizers—there were others like him at Youngstown," he said. "The place was a powder keg of troublemakers."

The boys set Calvin in one of the cells and stepped back. Calvin's tunic fell open, and Brian reached down to inspect something.

"Hey, look at this. It's one of Hamilton's dials."

"Ouch," said Peter. "They forced him to carry a message? Isn't that what those are for?"

"Ideally, yes. They're meant to be used on mages, though." McCracken shook his head. "Barbaric, but he brought it upon himself. Stupid boy."

"Do we leave it in?" asked Peter.

McCracken thought it over. "I'll interrogate him later, when I have time, and when he's more desperate. For now I must check on your sister. Brian, make yourself comfortable down here and keep watch over him. Peter, get the recruits to the dormitories. Give them the night off."

"Yes, Father," they both said. Brian locked the cell and sat on a bench against the wall. Peter followed McCracken upstairs and closed the brig door behind them.

As McCracken passed through the kitchen he nearly collided with Amelia, who had just come out of the storehouse with slices of peaches and cheese.

"Amelia! What are you doing?" McCracken asked.

"I'm sorry, I had to stock the storehouse alone today and I missed dinner. I remembered we had these, then I got hungry . . . sorry Dad, I'll put it back." Amelia turned to the storehouse door.

McCracken tried not to smile; Amelia couldn't have heard Calvin through the thick pantry walls.

"No, you don't have to do that. You just startled me, is all. Although . . ." McCracken reached for a slice of peach, draped a thin piece of cheese over it, and popped it in his mouth.

"It's good, isn't it?" Amelia smiled up at him. Damn, but she looked like her mother.

"Delightful. I should think it will be a national staple in a few years, love." McCracken patted her on the head and turned to leave.

"Dad, have you heard anything about Calvin?"

The question caught him off guard, and he was grateful for the low light in the kitchen. He knew his eye twitched when he lied to her. Maybe she wouldn't catch it.

"I told you Amy, he deserted a few weeks ago. Haven't gotten any news about him otherwise. Why do you ask?"

"I just, well, I could have sworn I heard his voice."

He hated seeing her sad. "Oh. That was just a messenger, coming in hot—he'd been cursed, like Badgett. Your brother

215

rushed him to the infirmary. Urgent news from Pittsburgh, no doubt. I suppose he does sound a bit like the Adler boy. Come here." He pulled her in and hugged her tight. "I know you hurt, but it's a childhood crush, nothing more. And it's a good thing Adler deserted when he did, so that you could see his true colors sooner rather than later. There are better men in the world, you know. You'll have your pick of them in years to come."

She sniffled and hugged him back. "Hmm."

"Go finish your treat, and take the evening off. I'll see you in the morning."

"Good night, Dad."

*

Godfrey's heart, mind, and soul worked in perfect harmony, like a living compass inside him, pointing him at Calvin Adler. He moved with swift purpose, crossing great distances at speeds previously impossible to him. It was as if the forces of destiny had gone on holiday, leaving him in charge in a way he'd never before experienced. Whatever debacle had caused him to wake up in the woods with new and amplified powers, it had been worth it. Calvin Adler's days were numbered.

Between Louisiana and, well, wherever he was headed, Godfrey used a long-neglected teleportal with the intent of staying dark on the grid. The monitoring agents paid more attention to the busy channels, but he knew of many portals that had been dormant for years. This particular jump moved him ninety miles, and the next portal from there was only three miles north. As fate would

A NEGLECTED TELEPORTAL...

have it, he was able to add to his arsenal along the way.

The portal dropped him outside an abandoned settlement overgrown with weeds, its buildings in utter ruin. It still showed evidence of a centuries-old fight, probably dating back to the quashing of the first Duffer Rebellion. That wasn't what called his attention to it, though: his senses detected something else—something new, deep within the ground. Like a blind man seeing or a deaf man hearing for the first time. He marveled at this aspect of his magic. As he had never felt this particular sense working within him, he stopped and puzzled it out in his mind until he figured out what it was.

Necromancy. A great and widespread death had taken place here long ago. The victorious mages had elected to slaughter the duffer traitors and bury them deep in the ground.

Traitors grave, he thought. He'd learned of them at Ipswich School. While the ringleader Washington had been worthy of execution via Draconic Trifecta in a public spectacle, his nameless supporters could be cast aside like the trash that they were, often by the hundreds. There were probably forty of these across the country.

Today they would serve a new purpose. *Godfrey's* purpose.

"History. Such a fascinating subject," Godfrey said. He knelt down and punched both fists into the soft earth, then closed his eyes and reached out with his untested necromancy. Back at Ipswich School, he'd learned how to hone a new magical discipline several times over, like developing a talent. It might take him a few tries to tune his instincts to a new brand of magic, but he could figure it all out.

He stayed there for the better part of an hour, muttering in Saxon and testing the reaches of his power, learning what it felt like to come in contact with something that had once been a human life. Yes . . . there was an excess of unruly souls down there, lingering around their bones, just waiting for him to come along and repurpose them according to his needs. Men, women, children, still wearing the clothes they had on when they'd been pushed into the afterlife. Godfrey called to them. They answered. They stirred, they pressed, they clawed their way up.

The ground surged, swelling in a few places, then rising everywhere, breaking up in great uneven clumps of mud and roots and whatever else had settled over time. He stepped back as the first hands broke through, finding purchase for the desiccated undead to pull themselves free, to do his bidding with what remained of their bodies.

After two centuries underground, they were mostly reduced to dark brown bones and tiny bits of flesh that had turned to hard leather at the joints. To Godfrey's amazement, the necromancy enchanted their bones, helping the skeletons to stand erect, move, and fight. The earthen smell of turned dirt brought with it the fetid scent of death, yet Godfrey only smelled the genesis of a new era.

It pleased him that his predecessors had thought to bury the duffers with their weapons.

*

THE GROUND SURGED...

The ripping headache did more to wake him up than the stabbing pain in his shoulders. He stood upright in the middle of a cell, arms tied above his head. Already he'd lost the feeling in his hands, and the numbness extended to his elbows.

Calvin coughed and regretted it right away, wincing at the intense throb on the right side of his skull. He wanted to cup a hand to his head, but his wrists were tied to opposite walls, keeping his arms spread wide. He felt worse than he had in days, and that was saying something.

The brig. He was back in the brig. Straw lined the floor; stone at his back, stone to either side, and iron bars in front of him. Brian sat on a bench outside the cell, humming to himself as he whittled away at a stick.

Calvin failed to bring a foul word to his lips. Knives jiggled around in his throat, or so it felt; he desperately needed water. The rasping sound that escaped his mouth caught Brian's attention, and the whittling ceased.

"Good morning. Well, afternoon by now—hard to tell down here. You've been out all day, thought you might have died. I was wondering what that would look like. I've never seen how it works," Brian said. He touched the tip of his knife to his own shirt, indicating Hamilton's dial. Calvin looked down at his tunic, which had fallen open, exposing the infernal contraption. The skin around it was pink, white, and green with infection, and it itched horribly.

Brian shrugged and resumed whittling. "I remember seeing a blueprint of it once. Eustice Hamilton designed it. You've met him, yeah? Good soldier, and most people don't realize he tinkers with the tech, too. He's pretty sharp. You should hear him go on about the human body, how it's just a machine like anything else. I'm trying to figure out how it draws electricity from your heart. And what will it do when the counter runs out? Guess we'll see, 'cause you've got less than an hour to go. Maybe if you have a *really* good reason for shafting the entire army and blowing the lid off the *Saint George,* we might pull it out of you."

Calvin's eyes drifted to the stairs. He couldn't take it anymore, being this close to Amelia, unable to reach her. Even if he had a voice there was no way she'd hear him down here. He'd blown it, blown his chance, after all that had happened. He should have stayed in the woods and waited for Amelia to do her chores out on the grounds. He'd had time. Why hadn't he waited?

He sniffed. Brian put down his stick and leaned in. "Oh man, are you crying? Ha! You're crying! Damn, but you're weak. And here I thought you might have been a half-decent warrior, beating me in a fight. Everyone will remember that as an accident now. Not that people will remember you—"

Two hands exploded out of the dirt wall behind him, clawing at the air and very nearly seizing the shoulders of Brian's field jacket. His battle-fast reflexes had him up on his feet, yelping in alarm. More arms emerged out of the soil all down the length of the wall, snaking out like tree roots. Hands, wrists, elbows . . . the wall bowed outward and entire sections of it broke away onto the stone floor. Then the skeletons came out.

Five, ten, a dozen of them, some taller than Calvin or Brian, others the size of children, tugged themselves loose, their jaws clicking hungrily, snapping all about. They were almost entirely reduced to bone, and threadbare clothing hung from their frames, all of it stained brown like dirt. Each of the undead had a glowing red light in its eye sockets, adding to their ghoulish appearance. In seconds the brig was nearly filled with them.

Brian's whittling knife flew from his hand and skittered between the bars. Fearing for his life, he drew his pistol and emptied the cylinder at the nearest skeleton with minimal success; though he shattered a few bones, the skeletons didn't seem to care. His final shot went straight through a skull, and that skeleton's red-ember eyes extinguished. It collapsed in a heap on the floor. The others seemed not to notice.

"Call them off!" Brian shrieked.

Coughing through the roughness in his throat, Calvin's immediate terror gave way to incredulity, and he managed a grim laugh. "You think they're with *me*? I have no idea—"

Brian didn't stick around to hear the rest. He flew up the stairs, and a second later the heavy brig door slammed shut behind him. The skeletons seemed inclined to let him go; all of their attention was on Calvin. They threw themselves viciously at the cell, reaching between the bars, desperate to grab him. He hung there, watching them struggle, and found that he was actually . . . unsurprised.

"This is not even the worst thing that's happened this week," he muttered.

The brig wall was dirt, but the cell was solid stone. As long as Calvin didn't go over to the bars, the skeletons couldn't touch him. He took a deep breath and considered his options. They were scant, but there was one way out of here.

The whittling knife.

Eyeing it like a coveted treasure, Calvin reached out with his leg and touched his toe to the handle, slowly dragging it closer. If only his hands weren't tied overhead . . . he craned his neck to see his wrists, trying to envision his next move. He sandwiched the knife between his heels, pressed them together, and tested the tenuous hold. It would have to do.

"Only one way this is going to work." He'd have to endure severe pain, have to dig deep to find the strength to pull it off, but what other option was there? Taking the ropes in his hands, he bit down hard and squeezed with all of his strength, hoisting himself a few inches off of the ground. He breathed out through his nose and pulled with his shoulders and sides, rolling backward in a controlled movement. As he went, he tucked his knees to his chest, hoping that he wouldn't drop the knife onto his stomach.

The hardest part was keeping enough pressure on it between his shoes as he extended his feet to where he could grab the knife with one hand. It took him three attempts, and when he finally got it, the effort had pulled two more hooks out of his chest, sending trickles of fresh blood down his front. This only made the skeletons more frantic. They grew in number, leaving Calvin to wonder just how many of them there were that he couldn't see.

He returned to the starting position and caught his breath. Then, holding his hand at an awkward angle, he sawed through the rope. His forearms burned, and he had to stop repeatedly lest he cramp up and drop the knife. Panting, he resumed the effort until finally the last strand parted, and his hand fell to his side.

Freedom. He'd have screamed with joy if he had the strength for it. He cut his other hand loose, rubbed the feeling back into it, and assessed his situation as the tingling faded away.

It was sloppy, but the skeletons had dug a quick tunnel to the brig from the front lawn. A lot of it had caved, yet behind the snapping throng he could see a glimmer of sunlight, and if he held his breath, he could catch faint echoes of . . . noise.

There was noise up top, the sounds of battle.

"What are you doing here?" he muttered to the skeletons. Who had sent them? And why had they let Brian go and instead focused only on . . .

No way.

The skeletons were the product of magic, and Calvin only knew of one mage who was after him. One mage who'd already survived something that should have killed him.

That was a grenade that missed. This time I knifed him right in the heart!

That damned Godfrey. Could it really be?

He had to get out of this cell.

Calvin stood back and studied the skeletons. The lights in their skulls were the most abnormal thing about them. Brian's words kept coming to mind, something about how the human body was a machine? Calvin had gotten pretty good at machines in a few weeks. Machines had weak spots . . . and Brian had supplied the secret to that as well.

"Here goes nothing." Calvin grabbed a skeleton's wrist and pulled it tight against the bars. The red light actually came from a glowing orb set in the hollow of its throat, which then shone out of its empty eye sockets. Aiming carefully with the knife, he stabbed at the red orb. It faded, flickered, and died. The skeleton collapsed just like the one Brian shot.

Got it. Calvin went to work.

*

With an army of animated thralls three hundred strong, Godfrey had marched to Virginia all night and all day, hopping through small teleportals to trim the distance. The advantage of the thralls was that they were all powered by Godfrey's life force, so anyone monitoring the portals would only sense one person inside.

And even if they could tell what was really going on . . . what could they do to him?

He came upon Mount Vernon in the late afternoon, a place Fitz's badge knew very little about. Godfrey couldn't be sure who lived here, only that Calvin Adler was on the grounds. There was so much frosted iron in the place that it was hard to get a feel, so he sent out thralls in groups of thirty to turn the whole estate on its head. Some had even burrowed into the ground at his suggestion that the building might have a basement.

Things were going swimmingly until a few dozen duffers

showed up and opened fire with black-powder weapons. Godfrey had completely failed to predict this turn of events. Technomancers? Right here, in Virginia? The nerve! He could think of four Corps outposts within a hundred miles in any direction, and the duffers had set up camp in the middle of them. Oh, these rebels had it coming.

Godfrey sent a necromantic command to his thralls: kill the technomancers. Stop their hearts from beating, and he could convert them into new thralls. That would turn the tide rather quickly. *Go forth and conquer!*

The skeletons obeyed. Though their primitive firearms had corroded, their blades and bayonets could still part flesh, and they used them to great effect while the technomancers reloaded. For their part, the duffers' weapons proved devastating: when their aim was good, they could cut down a thrall rather quickly, shredding his frail bones in a hail of bullets. Already, Godfrey counted nine thralls that had lost the use of their legs, and were dragging themselves bodily across the lawn to the duffers' various hiding places.

Then came something unexpected: somewhere in the melee, one of the duffers landed a shot on a thrall's neck. A critical hit! And it hurt almost as bad as if it had hit Godfrey himself. A wave of nausea shook him, and he no longer sensed that thrall. Where had it been?

Another shot rang out, this time close by, and Godfrey saw a second thrall stagger under the force of the weapon. Deprived of the power that had animated it, the skeleton fell to pieces, and Godfrey had to grit his teeth against the pain that shot up his own spine. Pawing at his throat as he drew breath, it occurred to him that even this new, powerful magic had its limits. A foreign sense warned him that he'd lose too much of his own life force if he wasn't careful.

He'd have to be more judicious with the thralls.

Godfrey drew his wand and aimed it at the fallen skeleton. *"Asprungnes cyme!"* This was the animator charm that he'd used in the first place; he figured it would work again, and in this he was disappointed. It seemed a corpse would only take his magic once.

"Bugger," he muttered.

Calling out to the others, he urged them to spread out and make harder targets of themselves. At the same time, he retreated from the frontlines to get a distant perspective on the battlefield, the better to redirect his thralls. He mentally steered them around obstacles so they could surround and isolate technomancers on the fringe, then pull them aside and kill them brutally. As soon as the duffers were down, he'd reanimate them with a flick of his wand; those recently turned were more resilient than their skeletal counterparts, and as Godfrey deployed them, he noticed that the living duffers were hesitant to open fire on their dead comrades.

Good! Now to get a better idea of the lay of the land. He singled out one of the duffers, a balding man who was dishing out orders to the rest, and sent the thralls after him. The thralls swarmed the man, killing him in seconds but carefully leaving his skull intact. Godfrey turned him. The duffer's knowledge pooled into Godfrey's mind, and from it he formed a map.

"Where are you hiding, Calvin?" Godfrey wondered aloud.

Stab.

His throat again! Godfrey coughed. Somewhere, a thrall fell. Then another. Then another. All in the same spot as the very first, somewhere underground, under the main mansion. Godfrey spat up blood. Consulting his map, he turned his attention to the basement. He had a feeling he knew who was down there.

We meet again!

*

With the last skeleton down, Calvin could focus on escaping. The knife was worthless as a lock pick, but one of the skeletons had brought a rusted rifle with a bayonet affixed to the end, which Calvin snatched up. Once he had popped the lock open, he swung the gate out and made his way to the stairs on shaky legs. It hadn't taken too long to down the skeletons; they'd seemed eager to get within stabbing range. By the time he was done, they'd actually blockaded the hole they'd dug to get in there. He was hesitant to consider himself fortunate by any means, but he was grateful for that development.

Of course, the door at the top of the stairs was locked. Having no other recourse, Calvin pounded his fists on it.

"Help! Somebody open the brig!"

Could anyone hear him? He was about to knock again when a jolt of electricity surged through his chest, driving him to his knees.

The device! It shocked him—a deep pain that he could neither abide nor ignore, more crippling than anything he'd endured on his run. This was horrendous. The shock came and went in the blink of an eye, yet an instinct warned him that there would be more to come. Burying his chin in his chest, he tried to read the dials in the low light; the "days" and "hours" had run out, and the markings on the "minutes" dial had been scratched and washed off in his travels.

Today is November the fifth. The tenth day, he thought.

He pounded the door for all he was worth, screaming until his throat could no longer make a sound. Down below, he heard the clacking and scraping of more skeletons digging through the collapsed tunnel.

Terrified, Calvin struck at the door again. It opened before he made contact, and he almost punched the person who had come to answer his call.

His eyes seized upon her face, daring his heart to confirm it.

There she was. Inches away.

Amelia.

He must have looked quite a mess, for she didn't immediately recognize him. Of course! He'd been in the sun for days, frozen and wind-whipped by night, cut, scratched, cursed, bludgeoned twice in the face—both recently and a ways back—and to top it off, he was wearing clothes that had never been his.

Even so, her beautiful eyes blossomed like sunflowers.

"It's . . . oh, it's you! Calvin!"

IT'S YOU!

He threw himself at her. She leapt into his arms with equal fervor and they squeezed with everything they had, giving into that precious release, saying through touch what they could never have said through words. For the first time in ten days, he didn't care about the thing in his chest, not even as she crushed it harder against his heart.

"They said you ran off!" she sobbed.

"They lied. Amelia, I—" He meant to warn her about the skeletons, but the device cut his words short. His scream startled her out of his embrace, and she pulled back as he fell to the floor. His senses failed him, save for his hearing, which keenly detected the thralls as they clamored up the stairs. Amelia, bless her, had the presence of mind to crouch down, hook her arms under Calvin's, and pull him out of the way while he pawed helplessly at the dial, attempting to breathe. Once she had him clear, Amelia shouldered the door closed and threw the bar across it.

The device calmed down again. Calvin spat blood onto the tile floor. With tears streaming down her face, Amelia helped him up. "What happened to you?"

"Later," he wheezed. "Those skeletons, are there more outside?"

"Yes, they're swarming the grounds! I've never seen anything like it. The others are holding them off and Dad has the house on lockdown. We have to go help him," she said.

Calvin grabbed her wrist. "No! Amelia, he . . . *aaargh!*" The intermission didn't last nearly as long this time. The device struck again, sending Calvin sprawling onto the floor.

AMELIA MCCRACKEN

CHAPTER 18

From within the cupola at the top of the mansion, Commodore McCracken took a quick survey of the incursion. The defenses were failing; whatever these creatures were, they cared not for bullets or grenades. The only thing that seemed to deter them was fire, a weapon the technomancers had in precious little supply. Worse, they had the power to turn their victims to their side; half of the recruits were now fighting against their fellows, bearing that hellish red light in their eyes. What brand of evil was this? He'd probably read about it before, but in the heat of battle he struggled to recall the nomenclature.

It wasn't important. McCracken had no intention of

surrendering his home, the war room of the revolution—not this afternoon, not ever. Despite his age and his handicap, he wasn't just a spectator in this fight.

The cupola, a domed room lined with windows on all sides, secretly doubled as a gun turret. He had a fully automatic fifty-caliber deck gun hidden under the floor, along with three crates of belt-fed ammunition and half a dozen grenades. He planted the tip of his cane against a button in the floorboard and watched as the planks slid away to reveal the machine. It rose up smoothly and locked into place, primed and ready for use. In sync with the floor panels, all of the windows slid down into the walls, leaving him with a mostly open panorama for picking targets.

McCracken took a moment to slip on a pair of asbestos gloves and some earmuffs—the fifty-cal could deafen a man permanently before too long. Then he started a full belt of bullets into the feed tray, pulled the handle, disengaged the safety levers, and stepped up under the shoulder harness. Down on the lawn, a cluster of hostiles advanced on a pair of recruits hiding behind a boulder. The recruits, occupied with reloading, would be ambushed in seconds.

"There comes a time when might makes right," McCracken said. Years had passed since he'd uttered those words; it was his battle cry. Pointing the muzzle through an open window, he lined up the sights and fired.

Bones and old flesh exploded out the backs of the attackers—skeletons, he realized. Walking skeletons? Some of their eyes dimmed too, or at least he thought so. He couldn't be sure, gazing

"MIGHT MAKES RIGHT..."

through the pungent smoke that belched out of the rotating chambers as the gun spat out empty cartridges.

The two recruits looked up at the cupola and saluted their Commodore, then shouldered their weapons and rejoined the fight. McCracken swept laterally and kept firing, maintaining a cadence of three to six shots per burst. As he spread the gunfire around the new targets, he spotted one walker among the rest who looked noticeably different: he was of whole flesh, though not a technomancer, and he moved with great agility. McCracken stopped firing long enough to realize that this one was giving orders. The skeletons obeyed him like a field commander. And for whatever reason, he didn't have that red light glowing in his face.

McCracken remembered now.

"Necromancer," he spat. It had been a long time since he'd even heard rumors of one of those. Death magic was one of maybe four disciplines that the Crown didn't openly cultivate—something about side effects on the user? This mage obviously didn't care.

That doesn't make him invincible.

McCracken lined up the crosshairs on the necromancer's chest—he was skinny, and he looked remarkably young. Age didn't necessarily matter in war; if the kid didn't want to get shot at, he shouldn't have attacked Mount Vernon. McCracken squeezed both triggers and lit him up.

A barrage of bullets ripped into the necromancer's ribs and stomach, shredding him instantly. The boy staggered and fell onto his back, his torso a ruined, bloody mess, and his skeletons—*thralls*, McCracken recalled the term—likewise staggered, their movements unsteady. There. Now the recruits could easily finish up the job! All in a day's . . .

The necromancer got back up.

"What?" McCracken aligned the sights again and gave the necromancer a second barrage, emptying the rest of the belt into him. Bullets pulped his flesh and splintered his bones; once again the boy went down, having been perforated through every major organ including his brain. Maybe McCracken had just missed the first time—and with the fifty-cal, of all guns! After the war, he'd have to get back on the range and . . .

Again the necromancer stood up, covered in blood, but whole.

McCracken swore under his breath. "You're not getting the message, are you?"

He fed another belt into the tray, pulled the handle and fired. This time the necromancer was prepared; he took off running in a zigzag formation, waving his arms about and shouting out defensive spells in Saxon, spells that had nothing to do with necromancy. McCracken's bullets ricocheted off of invisible shields, and at the same time, the necromancer's wounds simply disappeared, knitting into whole flesh like it was nothing.

McCracken's finger relaxed on the trigger and he lifted his gaze to peer over the barrel, stunned. Whatever this boy was, he couldn't be just a necromancer. This was new territory. Not even the greatest known sangromancers could heal so fast, while simultaneously erecting shield charms like that. It just couldn't be done—there was too much concentration and precision involved, especially for one so young! Where had this mage gotten such power?

The pause in his firing allowed thralls to push back against the recruits. Jolting back into action, McCracken pivoted the machine gun through a different opening and fired at a swarm of skeletons that had congregated on the south side of the house. He put down six or seven before they scattered like vermin, no doubt under the necromancer's direct command. McCracken emptied the second belt and was feeding in a third when out of the corner of his eye he saw Brian and Peter lead a contingent of recruits onto the roof of the barracks. Some of them carried rifles and were sharp-shooting the thralls in their throats. Each skeleton that they hit ended up falling to the ground, motionless, all traces of red light gone.

Across the front lawn, a slender figure staggered out from behind a wide tree. The necromancer! McCracken saw the movement out of the corner of one eye and in an instant he trained the machine gun on him. The necromancer thrashed about on the grass, grabbing at his own throat in obvious pain. McCracken's memories came back, reciting tidbits of knowledge from books read decades ago on the subject of magical balance. Powerful magic demanded a price from the user; necromancy brought life to the dead by borrowing it from someone else. In this case it was the necromancer himself.

McCracken shot the necromancer's thigh and knee; his femur exploded, and five nearby thralls fell as he recalled the necessary life force to speed-heal from his injuries. To slow him down, McCracken kept his finger on the trigger, spewing lead until the barrel thermometer screamed for him to stop. Swearing, McCracken let off and fanned smoke out of the air with a handkerchief, watching the necromancer to see if he got up.

He was distracted, and didn't notice a cluster of thralls scaling the mansion walls. One of them skittered up the angled roof and launched itself at McCracken, its bony fingers extended like daggers. McCracken saw it and feinted at the last moment, then made a fist and threw a pile-driver punch into its skull so hard that the brittle bone shattered. Its red light went out and McCracken quickly heaved the motionless skeleton back outside, only to be greeted by a second wave, some of them recently turned.

Brilliant strategy; surround him on all sides and turn the high ground into a death trap.

"Not today," he growled. Ignoring the mercury bubble, he got back under the shoulder harness, pivoted the gun and angled the sights to follow the roof's slope. Two quick bursts swept the thralls off the tiles, sending a cascade of bones to bury the next wave.

He didn't have time for this! McCracken looked back to the tree; the necromancer lay sprawled on the lawn, healing from a headshot that one of the recruits had inflicted on him. There had to be a breaking point, right? Magic had to be consciously controlled, so if they destroyed the brain, how could he heal? Unless death magic played by some other rules?

"Clearly I haven't shot you enough," McCracken said. He barely heard his own words through the earmuffs. Checking to be sure that he still had ammo, he opened fire yet again as the necromancer tried to stand up. Each bullet hit its target . . .

. . .and passed right through.

What?

The necromancer actually turned his head and smiled right at McCracken. His body remained whole; no rent flesh, no spraying blood. Like he wasn't even there.

Exactly like that.

241

Hellfire and damnation, he knew *psychomancy* too?

The mental illusion of the necromancer faded away, leaving a violently torn-up section of lawn where the technomancers had vainly concentrated their fire, all for nothing. The real necromancer's voice boomed in the darkness, though where he was, none could tell.

"I was wondering how long it would take you to figure that out!"

Chills ran down McCracken's spine as a flood of thralls engulfed the roof from every direction, having drawn near while he was focused on the psychomantic illusion. They moved like overlarge spiders, agile, fast, their eyes full with that awful glow. Ever the strategist, McCracken realized a horrible truth: if they turned him, if that necromancer added him to their ranks, he'd take everything McCracken knew about the army. The war would be over instantly.

This time, forever.

McCracken angled the gun to sweep again, but the thralls expected this and spread out. He destroyed a paltry few compared to the tidal wave surging upward; still he cleared them off and swiveled the gun in a tight circle, cupola walls be damned, firing at anything that moved. The belt ran dry, and the gun clicked on empty, echoing the noise of the incoming hostiles.

Dusk had fallen. McCracken cast his eyes about in the dark, looking for another belt, but he was out; the thralls closed in, pushed onward by their master's will.

This was it. McCracken looked across the yard at Peter, who

waved his arms frantically overhead. *Come, Dad,* he seemed to say. Other recruits tried to sharp-shoot the thralls, but there were too many. McCracken shook his head as the first skeleton came within arm's length. He knocked it aside. Another took its place. Then another. And another. The next thing he knew, his revolver was in his hand, the cylinder empty, with six downed thralls clogging the cupola. It wasn't nearly enough.

So this was how he would go out.

Setting his jaw, McCracken discarded the pistol and signaled Peter to execute a full-scale retreat. His eldest son froze with fear, and McCracken wished he could reach out to him, to lend him courage for what he was about to witness . . . but he had already done all he could to prepare his sons for the horrors of war. *Be brave, Peter.*

The thralls closed in. Several bony fingers stabbed through his thick clothes and penetrated his skin. The fiery prick of necromancy seared his flesh, but they were too late: McCracken drew a grenade out of the stock, pressed it to his chest, and pulled the pin.

"I'm coming home, Edith," he whispered, and released the grenade's spoon.

His final thought was a single line from his studies those years ago: a necromancer could only steal knowledge from a brain that was intact.

*

Once it was clear that the skeletons' goal was to surround the mansion, it only made sense to get out while they still could. Amelia knew what Dad would do: man the gun in the cupola and lay waste to the enemy.

However, when fighting magic, one couldn't rely on a single plan to win the day. If the skeletons overran the recruits, Dad would be trapped up there with no way out. Meanwhile Calvin was semi-lucid, murmuring incoherently about a pain in his chest.

She knew of one way to solve both problems. While the skeletons were still out front, she would leave through the back, get into the woods, and get Dad's mimic. It had a medical kit aboard for Calvin, and its thrusters could hover over a fixed object—perfect for extracting Dad. Even if Calvin could only control himself for a minute, he could man the weapons. While everyone else fought, she would provide a retreat option.

Amelia half dragged, half pushed Calvin into the woods, stifling the overwhelming fear that came with hearing so much gunfire. If they were still shooting, they weren't winning. Then, amidst all of the reports of black powder and lead, one roaring explosion dwarfed the rest. It was so loud that Amelia couldn't help but look back to see a giant cloud billowing out of the house, big enough to engulf the cupola and half the roofline.

No.

Maybe . . . maybe he'd set a trap? He had grenades up there, didn't he?

"Amelia . . ." Calvin moaned.

She didn't trust herself to speak. Had Mom been afraid like

this? On all of those missions with Jack Badgett, had she felt this kind of fear? The despair, the powerlessness that came with being on the losing side?

What would she have done?

One thing at a time, Amy.

Yes. One thing at a time. She said a quick prayer for Dad, threw an arm around Calvin, and continued onward. A minute later—two, tops—they reached the natural enclosure that concealed the mimic.

It was a unique model, based on a wyvern—sleek, fast, and heavily armed. It was also big, with a passenger bay and a cockpit, so they would be fully enclosed. She helped Calvin up the rear ramp, closed the hatch and led him to the copilot's chair where she strapped him in.

"We have to get as many of the others as we can. I don't know where Dad is, but my brothers will be at the barracks with the recruits," she said, flipping switches and rushing through the pre-flight steps. She'd practiced this countless times when Dad wasn't around, but she'd only ever gone through the motions. Hopefully she'd been doing it right.

"No . . . no . . ." Calvin muttered.

"Please Calvin, can you man the guns? I'll fly, you shoot."

"No use . . . undead. Waste of rounds," he said.

She disengaged the foreguns and armed the flamethrowers. "Then use these, and don't hit the barracks."

The wyvern ascended over the trees. So far, so good. She kept the jump-jets on and eased the boosters forward, turning the flaps to rotate in a slow portside circle. The mansion shifted into view, its walls dark with skeletons. The roof still burned. Not far off, her brothers stood on the barracks, no longer shooting back. Some recruits hurled grenades, but most everyone else had their daggers in hand as the skeletons surrounded the structure.

"Calvin! Come on!" Amelia pleaded.

With great effort, Calvin reached for the controls. She talked him through it as she flew; flamethrowers required no marksmanship, and the controls had stabilizers to steady the sweep. When she had them in range, Calvin spouted a stream of liquid fire at a clique of thralls near the stables. He worked the handles this way and that, laying down sloppy lines of fire on the grass. Amelia was about to ask what he was doing, but then it became clear: he'd created a path from the barracks into the woods, lined with fire, separating the skeletons from the technomancers.

"Brilliant," she breathed.

"*Damn it, aaaaargh!*" Calvin relinquished the controls and threw his head back against the seat, arching his spine and tearing at his shirt.

"Calvin!"

"Take . . . it out . . ." he panted.

Keeping one eye on the escaping recruits, Amelia reached over and pulled his shirt open.

Oh no.

The last time she'd seen that device, it was just a blueprint, a twisted invention of Eustice Hamilton. How had Calvin gotten one in his heart?

The spasm ended. Catching his breath, Calvin clamped his hands over the device like he wanted to tear it out but couldn't bring himself to do it. Amelia released his shirt and rotated the wyvern to bring the cupola into view, hoping against hope for some sign of her father.

Her hope died when she saw that the fire had eaten its way down through the second floor of the mansion. Smoke blackened the whitewashed walls and gushed out of open windows. Heaps of motionless skeletons lay at the base of each wall, their red lights gone. Of two things she was certain: Dad had been up there when it happened.

And he hadn't gotten out.

The smoldering mansion blurred as tears filled her eyes.

Gone, like Mom.

Out on the front lawn, a young man—a boy, even—climbed atop one of the boulders and watched the last of his skeletal army dance at the edges of the flames, unable to pursue the fleeing recruits into the woods. Peter and Brian would be with those recruits. They would survive, for a while at least. Under the guidance of her brothers, they'd probably even make it to the shark mimic, or to one of the nearest outposts. She was just about to bring the wyvern around and fly after them when Calvin screamed, coughed up blood, and fainted atop the console.

"Calvin? *Calvin!*"

No response.

The others would have to get by; Calvin needed her now, or that *thing* would kill him.

And she wouldn't lose him too.

*

Godfrey quickly learned the risks of abusing his power. Spreading his life force across the thralls was like drawing water from a cask and distributing it among so many cups, only the cask was his soul. Whatever the technomancers killed, that was one more cup that he couldn't return to the cask, and he was running dangerously low on power. Breathing deep to slow his frantic heart, he shut his eyes and sensed his remaining thralls, recalling the power back to him. Scores of skeletal bodies fainted on the spot, and when he had it back, he was surprised at how much he had lost.

What effect would that have in the long term? He didn't know. Perhaps it would shorten his life, or else make him easier to kill. Worse yet, there could be eternal complications, made all the more daunting because of what he didn't know. Of the many skills he'd mastered at Ipswich School, he had never learned much about necromancy. He needed to change that, and fast.

He surveyed the damage around him. The last of the technomancers disappeared into the trees, their shadows dancing in the firelight. That didn't concern him. What concerned him was the giant metal wyvern machine, not as large as the Youngstown dragon but still respectable. In his weakened state, Godfrey could barely detect Calvin Adler close by. Then the connection faded.

Bugger all. From a tactical standpoint he had won this battle, yet Adler once again eluded him. The urge to keep hunting him ate at Godfrey, and he hated to admit that in his present state, he was too weak to do so. The mimic fled into the darkness, beyond his reach. There would be another chance later, though.

For now, he would tend to the spoils of war. Using Birty's wand, he traced a circle of runes in the dirt, and when he finished, he plunged the wand into the center of it, driving it several inches down.

"*Acwencan!*"

It took a few minutes, but the fire died out, reduced to smoldering charcoals. Birty's wand burned up in the process, but Godfrey wasn't worried about it. He would get another wand.

Right now he wanted to see what else there was to learn about these duffers. Wobbling on unsteady legs, he walked to the house.

END OF THE ROAD.

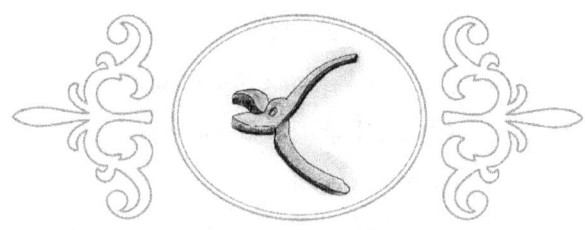

CHAPTER 19

When she could wait no longer, Amelia brought the mimic down at a place on the map called Huntley Meadows. The mud and soft grass helped to lessen the shock of a hard landing, and the outriggers dug three short trenches as they brought the mimic to a halt. The feet might be stuck, but she didn't care. Though she'd flown fast, they hadn't gone far. Calvin now lay screaming on the floor, rocking from side to side.

Amelia sprang out of the chair and opened a cabinet in the back where Dad kept the toolbox. She hauled it back to Calvin, and fished around inside for a screwdriver and a pair of pointed pliers. Once she had them, she took two fistfuls of Calvin's shirt and ripped it wide open.

"Move your hands!"

He couldn't, so she had to force them apart and pin them to his sides. With no other recourse, she straddled his torso to hold him still. He arched his back again, eyes shut, lips peeled back, and teeth clenched. Spittle and sweat seemed to fly from everywhere on his face, and his breath was ragged. Stifling a whimper, Amelia bit her lip and pressed the flat head of the screwdriver into a slot on the side of the dial. Calvin twitched, and the movement caused another hook to rip his skin—half of them were out now, and the dial was dangerously loose. Dark red blood filled the wound.

"Calvin, you have to hold still!"

"I! CAN'T!" He struggled to free his hands, and she squeezed her legs tighter to keep his arms down. Mercy, but he was strong! She couldn't do this for long.

There was no time left—this thing was killing him, sparking audibly every few seconds. Uttering another silent prayer, she went to work with the screwdriver and the pliers. Behind the clockwork face of the device would be a master pin that was supposed to defuse the thing. The drawing she'd seen must have been for a previous version though, because when she popped the face off, this device had no such pin. If she'd had another minute, she might have made sense of it, but with Calvin on the brink of death, she could only think of one other thing.

She grabbed a second set of pliers, took one in each hand, and held them above the heads of the nails in his heart.

"Calvin . . . I love you, okay?" She clamped the pliers into place.

252

"AAARGH!"

One. She breathed in deeply and held it.

Two. Her lungs held her own thundering heart steady.

Three!

She pulled. Every last inch of steel came out, dragging thick blood and slime behind it.

Calvin's howl stung her ears. As the nails came free, the device fired its failsafe mechanism, pumping the last of its positive charge through one nail and using the other as a negative pole. A small crack of lightning shot between the two tips, shocking her hands and filling the air with a terrible odor. She yelped and dropped everything; the tools clanged against the metal floor.

Then all was silent, save for the ringing in her ears and the diminishing cadence of Calvin's labored breathing. His skin glistened with sweat, then turned white and clammy to the touch, save for the deep holes where the nails had been. These filled with dark blood that oozed up and out. With a final *click,* the teeth that lined the device's edge retracted back into its underside. Disgusted, she batted the thing away, unable to imagine such a hellish thing buried over her own heart.

Keep treating him, she thought. He needed aggressive medical attention; infection was his worst enemy now. The trauma site was a horrible mess of blood and flesh that needed serious treatment, or else it would turn gangrenous. For now, the immediate concern was bandaging the wound and covering him with a blanket; he'd soon go into shock.

A quarter of an hour went by in relative silence while she sponged blood and pus out of the wound and applied an antiseptic, followed by a clotting agent. She stuffed the whole of it with gauze and secured the bandage with tape. Unfortunately the medical kit didn't have any tobacco leaves, or she could have used them to treat the bruises on his face; a yellowing spot on the bridge of his nose might have been more than a week old, while a fresher, purple mark colored the side of his head.

"You're going to be all right, Cal," Amelia whimpered. For now, she'd done all she could. Calvin's breathing and pulse had stabilized, and he slept.

Heaving a sigh of relief, Amelia wiped away a tear and pressed the back of one hand to her mouth, trying not to think of all that had happened in the last hour. Of all that she'd lost.

Dad. Peter. Brian. Home.

But Calvin was here.

An hour ago she thought she'd never see him again. Now they were lost together, and a cruel reality awaited them outside the mimic.

Amelia took Calvin's hands in hers, drawing what comfort it offered. She wanted so desperately to talk to him, to know what had happened and where he'd been and how he'd ended up in the brig again. It would all have to wait. When he awoke, they would talk, and they would figure out where to go from there.

Because she had no idea what to do next.

*

NO IDEA WHAT TO DO NEXT...

A stream of sunlight pierced the cockpit window and hit Calvin's eyelids. He stirred.

"Amelia?" He could barely talk, and everything in his body begged him to be still. At least his bed was comfortable, whatever it was.

Amelia appeared at his side. Their hands found each other's without a sound. Her eyes were red and puffy, but she had that beautiful smile on her face, and he sagged in relief at her presence.

"Hi," she whispered.

"Hi," he said back. He poked at his chest with his fingers. A large bandage covered a tender wound. The device was gone!

"I took it out," she explained.

"Of course you did." He stroked her face with his hand. "How did you do it?"

"A little brutishly," she confessed. She told him how she'd seen a schematic for the device in a notebook that Hamilton had given to Brian. Calvin flushed with anger at the mention of their names.

"Hamilton tried to kill me. He put that thing in personally."

She stared at the device, sitting on a countertop opposite them. "I never thought . . . I mean I knew he was violent, I just can't see how he could do *that* to someone. I never knew he had that in him."

Calvin positioned his elbows beneath himself and held his breath, trying to sit up. "He wanted to keep you from me."

Her eyes drifted back to his. "That would never have worked, Cal."

Privately he was thrilled to hear her say that, just as an extra confirmation that her alleged betrothal to Hamilton was only so much blown smoke. He wasn't done with Eustice Hamilton, not by a long shot. "He'll get his," Calvin said.

She chewed her lip and stared off at nothing. Her free hand rested on one side of his chest, away from the bandage.

"I cleaned it," she said, sensing his question. "Be glad you were out, because it took a lot of alcohol. We'll have to watch it for the next week. You'll have scars for the rest of your life."

"Don't care about that." He took her hand again. "Amelia, where are we?"

"North of Virginia. We sort of crash-landed so I could take care of that thing, and I thought it best that we get going from there. Whoever attacked Mount Vernon did a pretty thorough job. It's all gone, and I don't know where my brothers took the recruits. If my orienteering is right, we're in the New Jersey province. There's a place I know outside Philadelphia where we can stay long term, I was just too tired to fly us there last night."

"Would you please help me up?"

She slipped her hands behind his shoulders and pulled him upright. Before he sat back against the bulkhead in the wyvern's sleeping quarter, she leaned in close for a hug, burying her cheek against his neck. His let his arms drape around her and gave her a gentle squeeze, holding her close to remind himself that yes, she was real. Her embrace told him that she needed that same confirmation.

"Thank you, for all of this. You saved my life," he whispered.

"You saved my brothers, and those recruits."

He stiffened at that.

"Cal, I know you didn't get along with them, but they're all I have left. Dad, he . . ." she choked on her words, and became silent. She didn't need to say more.

"I'm sorry. I'm so sorry. I don't know how to say this, Amelia: there was some trouble in Ohio, where your father sent me. I went under a false pretense. He tried to lock me up there, basically. And then I tried calling you on a HAM radio, and it all went downhill from there."

Amelia frowned. "Dad said you'd deserted." As soon as she said it, a horrific recognition dawned on her face.

"Technically I did, after *this* happened." He pulled back and tapped his chest. Amelia took his hand again.

"Don't touch it too much. You need your rest," she said. "And it seems like we have a lot of catching up to do."

"You said it. I don't even know where to start."

"Well, I can start with the bad news."

"More bad than what we just went through?"

She pursed her lips again, a signal that she was about to say something that she didn't want to be true. "We're in trouble, Calvin. Not just the technomancers, I mean all of us Merykans. The British are dead set on wiping us out after what happened at Camp Liberty—I heard Dad talking about it with Peter and Brian. A messenger came last week."

"That's old news. For all their faults, the technomancers have no shortage of firepower. You ever heard of the *Saint George*?"

"Whatever it is, it won't be enough," Amelia insisted. "King George sent reinforcements. Redcloak Elites, a contingent of Scottish Highlanders, and mercenaries from a place called Hesse. I don't know what they do but it sounds bad. Dad was nervous. Calvin . . . they're ready for us. Dad wanted to attack them tomorrow, but even if we could, they know we're coming.

"I don't know if we can win this anymore."

*

What a shame. The mansion had boasted an extensive library before it burned to the ground. The duffers had even acquired books on magic that were hard to get back in Britain; no wonder their tinkering had improved so much in recent generations.

Godfrey poked through the ashes, perusing the titles that had survived the conflagration; he couldn't pass up a chance to gaze into the duffers' minds by seeing their stronghold. Vulgar as they were, perhaps there was merit in studying their methods of combat. He had never learned such things back home.

Home. What an arbitrary term. Was Britain still home? Did he really want to go back, while so much untapped potential was staring him down on this side of the pond?

He examined a slightly burned map on the wall, its edges blackened by soot. The western half detailed the Merykan colonies, the Atlantic dominated most of the eastern half, and the British Isles resided at the very edge, nestled above France.

What was so great about the Isles? Cold, rainy, miserable all the time . . . on the other hand, Meryka was a vast wilderness, an expanse of endless possibilities. The Isles had no shortage of bickering politicians, of stuffy nobles jockeying for power and favor in the court of a corpulent inbred king.

It was a game he had no inclination to play, not after seeing his father contend all of his life only to become the Minister of Transcontinental Teleportation. In this land, Godfrey hadn't just honed his skills, he'd gained new magic. If he could scamper over hill and vale, get knocked unconscious, lose two days of memory, and come out on the other side with an inhuman combination of powers, what else could he do here?

"Don't make much sense to go back, does it?" he mused aloud, shelving a half-burnt tome. Let the King's toy soldiers fight each other for a higher spot on the shelf; Godfrey could stay far away from all of that over here, and be the smartest fox in the world, ruling the roost of hens.

Plenty of space, food, and opportunity.

Of course there'd be challengers; there always were. If he were to take over the Merykan colonies, he'd have to be fast and decisive about it. Shock and awe, as it were. Storm Vauxhaul Outpost, overwhelm the House of Commons, close off the teleportals, and seize control of the continental lodestone . . .

"Well, damn me blind. I could actually *do* all of that now." He studied the palms of his hands, then turned them over to admire the intricate details of the wasp tattoos on his knuckles. He'd

I WILL RULE THIS LAND.

stomped out a technomancer outpost in under an hour using only necromancy and psychomancy. He hadn't even tapped the pictomancy! Oh, there was so much left in the world for him to do. He couldn't possibly go back to the way things were.

That settled it. This was just a test run, a way to stretch his legs and showcase his talents.

I am unstoppable now. Sod the homecoming; I will rule this land instead. The mages will bow and the duffers will fall. Once it's all said and done, I will build a new throne on this continent, and before his life is over, King Charles will swear fealty to the Norrington Crown.

A thought occurred to him. *I will put the 'god' in 'Godfrey.'*

He grinned, studying the map for a long, long while.

END BOOK TWO

WAR HITS THE HOMELAND!

Calvin, Amelia, and the Rebel Hearts will return in

ENGINES OF LIBERTY:
PATRIOT'S GAME

Coming soon!

TACKLED MEN GOWNS!
(ACKNOWLEDGMENTS)

During the summer of 2013, when I was only a few short months into my career as a long-haul truck driver, I experienced my first DOT Crackdown. It's a border-to-border, coast-to-coast event where the governments of the USA, Canada, and Mexico all get together and spend three days over-citing truckers for violations. Cha-*ching* for them.

At the time, I worked for Knight Transportation. Their policy regarding the crackdown was that if there was anything more than slightly wrong with your truck, you stayed at a terminal and got it fixed. My truck had an issue with one axle which caused all four tires on it to wear irregularly, so like a ton of other drivers, I got stuck in Denver waiting for the backlogged mechanics to get to it. Rather than waste those three days with a bunch of sweaty dudes in the lounge watching *Swamp People* marathons, I sat in my truck and outlined *Engines of Liberty* in its entirety.

It took me less than a month to hammer out a complete draft of REBEL HEART. It went very fast, but it was designed that way; I wanted to put out a trilogy of light novels that wouldn't take too long to read. Just something to get me in the game. Within a year of that happening, REBEL HEART was fully edited, illustrated, and published, and I was well into SUICIDE RUN, the first sequel I've ever really written.

REBEL HEART had a lengthy acknowledgments section,

dedicated to the people who critiqued it and made it better. Honestly that list of people hasn't changed much for SUICIDE RUN, as they've all formed a sort of brain trust on the series. **Savannah** and **Shantewa** offered some helpful notes especially, and of course **Emily** and **Holly** nailed the edits. To cap it off, **Carter** once again proved his chops as a cover artist.

But the most serendipitous feedback came from my mother, who read a version that still had some of my older notes in it; in particular, there was a scene that referenced Amelia's mother, and I put in a note about how I still needed to select a name for her. Later I would choose the name "Edith", without telling anyone (because it didn't matter...just a minor detail.) After Mom's notes came back, she suggested "Edith", and when I looked at my working copy of the manuscript, I kind of laughed, because I'd already made that selection. Good old **Mom**.

(Her name's not "Edith", if you were wondering.)

So you see how making these books has kind of been a magical process; what you might not see is how horribly exhausting it is. The stress of creating a world and fixing it on paper can only be known by those who have attempted it, or their families. I don't say it enough, and maybe I don't express it properly, but I'll always be grateful to my wife **Schaara** for her support in this. Putting up with my multipolar behavior when I'm in "hardware mode" isn't easy, and that was especially true with this book, as she became pregnant with our second son while I was halfway through the illustrations. She is strong in ways that I'll never match, and this book might not have happened without her. I love you, babe.

The two unique names that I can add to this section are **Jenn Johansson**, who gave me a few pointers at WesterCon 67. She then introduced me to **Michelle Argyle**, who was kind enough to read REBEL HEART and make formatting suggestions that greatly improved the aesthetics of these last two books. Ladies, I owe you one. (Apiece, I suppose…I won't make you share.)

And of course, I would be horribly remiss if I did not thank *you*. Even if I didn't publish, even if nobody read my books, I would still write and I would still draw. I don't think I could give that up. I love it too much. In fact, I want to be able to do it full-time someday, and in order for that to happen, readers like you are crucial. I appreciate you purchasing this book, or checking it out, or borrowing it, and taking the time to read it. I hope you liked it.

And if you hated it, write a hilariously vicious review online somewhere. You'll go viral, and people will snatch up *Engines of Liberty* just to see if it's really *that* bad. We all win.

All joking aside though, I really mean that: thank you. Someday you'll be the reason why I don't have to drive a truck anymore.

Until then, well, enjoy the ending!

Graham Bradley, February 2015

About the Author

Graham Bradley began writing at the age of 8, and it's been a bad habit ever since. He enjoys cars, history, the Indianapolis Colts, BBQ, reading, and traveling. He currently lives in Henderson, Nevada, with his wife and son.

SUICIDE RUN is his second published book.

(If you get in a fight with a honey badger, my money's on you.)

Twitter.com/GrahamBeRad

Instagram.com/GrahamBeRad